CARING FOR CHRISTMAS

THE AMISH QUILTING CIRCLE

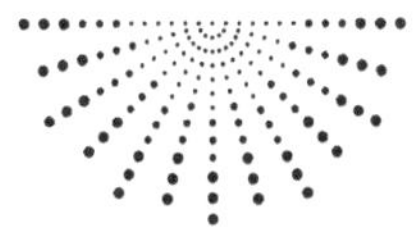

SARAH MILLER

IRENE GLICK

SWEETBOOKHUB.COM

WELCOME TO THE AMISH QUILTING CIRCLE

What is more lovely than a quilting circle? Good friends come together to drink coffee, eat cake, talk and work on a quilt or two. It is a wonderful way to spend an afternoon being both productive and having fun.

Only, this quilting circle likes to do a little matchmaking along with the quilting.

Join the ladies of Faith's Creek as they see who they will match next.

All the books are sweet and family-friendly with no nasty surprises.

If you missed the first book, you can grab An Englischer's Folly here.

If you are not already a member of my reader's news-letter, join here, for free, to be the first to find out when new books are released and for occasional free content.

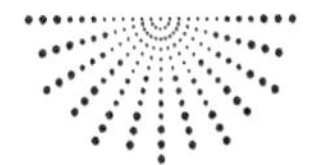

CHAPTER ONE

FAITH'S CREEK, PENNSYLVANIA.

"And it's my great privilege – and pleasure – to declare the two of you husband and *fraa*," Bishop Beiler said, closing his prayer book, as Barbara and Elijah shared a kiss.

Miriam Esch smiled, and her *mamm* slipped her hand into hers and squeezed it.

"Isn't it wonderful? Your sister looks so happy, Miriam," Lavinia whispered, as the bride and groom walked arm in arm along the aisle of the barn, where upturned hay bales had served as seating for the happy occasion of Barbara and Elijah's wedding.

It was a warm summer's day in Faith's Creek, and despite the Eschs being relative newcomers to the district, a *gut* number of people had turned out to witness that happy occasion. Miriam was sitting between her *mamm* and *daed* at the front of the barn, and they rose to their feet and followed the bride and groom out into the open air of the farmyard. The barn had been kindly lent by one of the farmers whom Thomas, Miriam's *daed* had become friendly with, and a large awning had been set up between three apple trees, under which a table, groaning with food, stood waiting.

"Wasn't that a lovely service?" Susanna Bontrager, Elijah's *mamm*, said, coming up to greet the new members of her family.

"I had tears in my eyes the whole time. It was just beautiful," Barbara's *mamm* said, as Elijah's two *kinner* – the twins, Saul and Elizabeth – ran past them towards the refreshments.

A lavish spread had been prepared, and after Bishop Amos Beiler had said grace, the guests tucked into a splendid feast. Miriam looked around her at the other guests, as she sat with her *mamm* under the shade of one of the apple trees. The quilting circle – of which her *mamm* was now a prominent member – had all turned up, along with friends of Elijah. In fact, as was tradition, the whole of the district, or at least those who could spare the time, had turned out for the celebrations. It was a sizable crowd.

Miriam was pleased for her sister. Barbara had not had an easy time in coming to Faith's Creek – an accident back in Idaho had confined her to the house in the run up to Christmas, and she had been lucky in meeting Elijah in the way she had done. The two of them had grown ever close as the early months of the year had passed by, and they had announced their intention to marry at Easter.

"It'll be strange not having Barbara at home, won't it?" Miriam said.

She knew she would miss her sister, whom she had been used to doing everything for in the aftermath of her accident. They had their tensions – just as any sisters do – but Miriam loved Barbara dearly, even as she knew things could not always remain the same.

"I don't think I'll ever get used to it. But she'll not be far away, and I've not yet lost you both, have I?" Miriam's *mamm* replied.

Miriam shook her head. She had no plans to marry, but Barbara's betrothal to Elijah had made her think more about the possibility. Her sister was pretty, resourceful, and determined. Miriam had always felt as though she lived in her shadow. Whatever she did, she always compared herself to her older sister, and that comparison always fell short.

Miriam glanced at Barbara, who was sitting with Elijah and the twins at a table on the far side of the awning. They looked like the perfect family, even as Miriam knew there was heartache there, too. Elijah had lost his first wife, Diana, and the twins had been left without a *mamm*. But Barbara would be everything they needed – Miriam had no doubt of that. Her sister looked beautiful – her long black hair tied back and covered with her *kapp*, her bright blue eyes ever smiling, and her rosy cheeks like those of their *mamm*, made Miriam feel second best. Her own hair was not as long, her eyes not as bright, her cheeks not as rosy.

"Am I to stay at home forever, *Mamm*?" Miriam asked, not meaning to sound so despondent, but the words had just come out.

Her *mamm* looked at her sympathetically and shook her head. "*Nee*, Miriam. That's not what I expect. A *mamm* needs to realize she'll lose her daughters – or her sons – one day. It's all part of growing up. A *rumspringa* prepares you for it. But marriage... that's when it really happens. Barbara and Saul are beginning a new life together now. They've made their vows and are blessed by *Gott*. That's the order of things, isn't it? Your turn's coming, I'm certain," her *mamm* said.

She put on a smile, but Miriam felt far less certain.

Since their arrival in Faith's Creek, Miriam had struggled to make friends. She had acquaintances – the women of the quilting circle – and those she met at the biweekly service. But that was all they were. She had been so focused on taking care of her sister, she had neglected her own happiness for the sake of Barbara and her health. But Barbara's injuries were healed, and now she was married, she no longer needed a nursemaid to follow her around and take care of her.

"Do you really think so? I've not had much luck, have I?" Miriam replied, pushing away her plate with a sigh.

Her *mamm* turned to her with a sympathetic look on her face.

"A wedding makes us think about these things. It puts them into focus. But you've got lots going for you,

Miriam. You're a lovely person. You're kind, considerate, and intelligent – think of all those books you read, just like your sister. Any man worth his salt would want to get to know you better. Just give it time, and trust in *Gott*. Forcing these things doesn't normally work," her *mamm* replied.

Miriam knew her *mamm* was trying to reassure her, but she still felt a sense of despair at the sight of her sister so happy, as she knew herself to be so sad.

"But I just don't know what I'm doing wrong," she persisted.

"You're not doing anything wrong, Miriam. But you know what your problem is, don't you?" her *mamm* replied, in a somewhat exasperated tone.

Miriam shook her head, feeling confused as to what her *mamm* meant.

"I don't know what you mean," she replied.

Her *mamm* rolled her eyes. "You've got far too much time on your hands, Miriam. When we came to Faith's Creek, you were looking after Barbara, and you did a wonderful job of that. But she's better now – she was better months ago. And she's a married woman. She doesn't need a nursemaid anymore. That leaves you with nothing to do. You're bored, and you're dwelling on the fact that you're not married. I know I'm your *mamm*, and I should want you to get married – but it's not the be-all and end-all, Miriam. Family, friends, hobbies, a job – those things matter, too," she replied, giving an encouraging smile.

Miriam felt guilty. She had not meant to be so self-indulgent. This was meant to be the happiest of days, and she knew she was spoiling it by being moody. She glanced again at Barbara, who was now surrounded by members of the quilting circle, who were offering their congratulations. She sighed and nodded.

"I'm sorry, *Mamm*. I just think about it, that's all. Barbara looks so happy, and I feel... left behind," she said.

Her *mamm's* look of exasperation turned somewhat more sympathetic, and she took Miriam's hand in hers and squeezed it.

"She's older than you. It was only right she got married first. It's not always the way, but it usually is. You're not being left behind. There're lots of things you could be doing – not just moping over not being married with six *kinner*. There're days I wish I had your freedom," her *mamm* replied.

Miriam nodded. She knew she needed to be better at being thankful for the things she had. Bishop Beiler had preached a powerful sermon on the subject, and Miriam had felt as though he were talking directly to her. But try as she might, those thoughts of discontent had prevailed, and the day of Barbara's wedding had brought them to the fore.

"I'm sorry, *Mamm.* I know I've got everything I need, but I just can't help dwelling on the matter," Miriam replied.

"You need a hobby. Why don't you come to the quilting circle again? You liked it when you came before."

Miriam felt another twinge of guilt. She had told her *mamm* how much she had enjoyed attending the quilting circle, and she had done so diligently for several months, even as her attendance had dwindled of late. But the truth was, Miriam detested quilting. She was constantly pricking her fingers, and whilst the other women produced the most remarkable designs, Miriam's own efforts were somewhat lackluster.

"I don't know... I'm not very *gut* at it, *Mamm,*" she said, shaking her head.

"You'll never be *gut* at anything if you don't try it for more than a few months. Don't you think a marriage takes effort, too?" her *mamm* replied.

Miriam nodded. Her *mamm* was right. She would never master anything if she did not put in the effort required. There was the matter of a job, too. Miriam had never had a job. At twenty years old, she had never had need of one, but now the matter seemed more pressing.

"I know, *Mamm*. I just..." she replied, glancing up across the farmyard.

By the far wall, three chicken coops stood. The hens were scratching in the ground, and a sudden thought occurred to Miriam, one which made her laugh out loud, even as her *mamm* looked at her in surprise.

"What's brought that on?" her *mamm* asked, sounding bemused.

"I've just had an idea – I'm going to keep chickens, and I'm going to sell the eggs at the market," Miriam replied.

Her *mamm* looked at her in astonishment.

"But you don't know the first thing about chickens," she exclaimed.

Miriam smiled. "Precisely. It's something entirely new. Something I'll have to work hard at. A quilt can be stuffed into a cupboard and forgotten about. But I can't do that with hens now, can I?" she replied, feeling suddenly very pleased with herself.

It might have seemed an astonishing idea, but the thought of it made Miriam feel extremely happy, and with her resolve in place, she felt as though she had finally found a purpose.

CHAPTER TWO

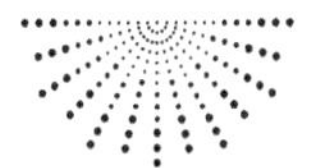

"Come on, Mildred, into the shed with you. Don't you want to stay warm for the night? I know I do," Miriam said, as she held up a sheet of corrugated iron, trying to herd the last of her hens into the shed at the far end of the garden.

It was late November, and snow had fallen on Faith's Creek that day. The hens had been surprised by the blanket now covering their scratching ground, and Miriam, too, had been taken by surprise. She had hurried to put fresh straw into the shed and was worried about the chill of the night to come. Winters could be harsh in Pennsylvania, and she had not worked so hard over the past few months to lose her flock to the chill of an icy night. She had two dozen birds – all good layers – and their eggs had proved popular at market. Miriam was proud of herself, and she had plans to increase her flock and make a name for herself by selling eggs to the community.

"Come on inside, Miriam. It'll be dark soon," her *daed* called out from the porch.

"I'm coming. I'm just getting Mildred inside. She's not budging," Miriam called back, as she tried to coax the last hen towards the shed door.

Eventually, Miriam snatched up the hen with a sudden deft movement, placing her firmly into the straw and closing the shed door behind her. It was far from adequate lodgings for her flock – the shed having previously been used for storing wood. But Miriam had not entirely appreciated the steep learning curve involved before acquiring her chickens, and the last few months had seen both triumphs and failures in her attempts to rear her hens and make them profitable.

"It looks like we're in for more snow. I'm glad I got all that wood chopped last month," her *daed* said, as Miriam hurried up onto the porch.

"I feel sorry for the hens. They're in that cold, draughty shed, and it's only going to get worse," Miriam replied, pulling off her outdoor boots and following her *daed* into the warmth of the parlor.

"Chickens are hardy birds, it is fine for them," he said.

Miriam knew he was right but she wanted something better. She even realized that the hens needed air, an airtight coop would be worse than this.

Her *mamm* was in the kitchen, and the pleasant smell of roasting chicken – not one of her own – filled the house. Miriam was hungry, but she could not help but think of the chickens and how cold they would be that night.

"Well, there's the chicken coop out there. Why don't you fix that up for them?" her *daed* said, looking at her scowl.

Miriam had not thought of that. The chicken coop was a remnant of a previous owner's occupation. It was run down and had no roof. But if she could repair it, it would provide a far better shelter for the hens in the coming months. It stood against the side wall of the house, protected from the worst of the prevailing weather, and would be far easier to secure against predators than the shed, from which she had already suffered the visit of a fox.

"That's a great idea, *Daed*," she said, beaming at him.

He laughed. "I have them sometimes. Come on. Let's get washed up. I could eat a horse – let alone a chicken," he said.

That evening, Miriam made plans for the repair of the chicken coop. She was not the most practical of people, but she was always willing to have a go, and whilst carpentry was not her forte, she had seen her *daed* working in his tool shed often enough to believe she knew what was required.

"Wood and nails, I suppose," she told herself, setting off the next morning in the direction of the mercantile.

The hens had been fine in the night, but she decided they were grumpy – if hens could be said to be grumpy – though she had to admit that there was no evidence of this when she had put down their corn that morning. Miriam knew it was not fair to see them remain in the shed, when a perfectly good chicken coop stood waiting to be prepared. The mercantile was the sort of store that sold everything, and Miriam looked around it with interest, trying to work out what precisely was required.

"Can I help you, miss?" the store clerk – a young man with tousled blonde hair and pimpled cheeks – asked.

"Oh, yes. I'm doing... some woodwork. I need wood and nails," Miriam replied, knowing she sounded somewhat vague.

It was her sister who was skilled in practical tasks. Barbara would have known precisely what to ask for. But Miriam was confused.

"What length of wood? I can cut it for you. And the size of the nails? Are you just hammering them in, or do you actually need screws?" the clerk replied, fixing Miriam with a questioning look.

Miriam faltered. She had not made any measurements, even as she realized how foolish she had been in not doing so. As for nails – did they not come in one size only?

"Well... just wood, planks. It's to mend a chicken coop," she replied, realizing again the folly of her words.

Chicken coops did not come in standard sizes, and the clerk gave her an exasperated look.

"I can cut the wood for you. But it comes in a certain length. Have you got a buggy with you – to carry it, I mean?" he asked.

Miriam shook her head. She had not thought of that, either. Her *daed* would gladly have accompanied her, but Miriam had wanted to do things alone. She had wanted to prove herself, even as she was proving herself a fool. At that moment, she noticed a man watching her from along the aisle. He was a little older than she – perhaps twenty-two or twenty-three – with red hair and bright blue eyes. Miriam blushed under his gaze, and to her surprise, he stepped forward and smiled.

"I couldn't help overhearing what you were saying. It's all right, Fletch, I think I know roughly the measurement the lady needs," he said.

The store clerk nodded, and the man explained what was required, and informed Miriam she would need the packet of nails he indicated, along with one or two other things she had not thought of. The store clerk cut the wood and bundled it together, tying it in such a way so that Miriam could drag it along through the snow. She felt very grateful to the other man for his help, though she was still embarrassed at her lack of practical knowledge.

"Is there anything else?" the store clerk asked, and Miriam shook her head.

"No, that's all, *denke*. You've both been very kind," she said, glancing at the red-haired man, who smiled at her and nodded.

"I hope you manage to make your repairs. I'm sure you will," he said, and blushing, Miriam hurried out of the store.

"They must think I'm a helpless little damsel," she thought to herself, even as she knew she was far from that.

Miriam hurried home through the snow, eager to begin the repairs immediately. She had brought more wood than she needed, knowing she was bound to make mistakes, and enough nails to lose half of them in the snow – which she was certain she would do. But despite feeling somewhat foolish, Miriam still felt proud of all she had achieved. The hens were her pride and joy, and she would build them a hen coop worthy of her own achievements.

"But I wish I'd asked his name," she thought to herself, as she returned home that afternoon.

As she went about her repairs – or the attempt at them – Miriam could not help but think of the young man who had helped her. She did not know his name, but she knew one thing for certain – she would not forget his smile.

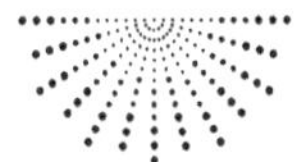

CHAPTER THREE

"Poor kid, she didn't have a clue what she needed, did she?" Fletch Pollock said, shaking his head, as Paul Abrams paid for his purchases at the counter a few moments after the young woman who had experienced so much confusion over what lengths of wood to buy, had left.

Paul shook his head and smiled.

"We've all got to learn at some point. There're not many women who'd set foot in here asking for wood, let alone buy it and take it home to repair a chicken coop," he replied.

He had been intrigued by the woman. She was very pretty, and he was surprised he had not seen her before.

Paul was often at the mercantile store. He worked as a carpenter, repairing furniture in his own workshop, and the mercantile was the place he came to buy the materials he needed for his work.

"I've never seen her before, either," Fletch replied, as Paul handed over his money and took up his purchases.

"Well, I hope she manages to repair her chicken coop. It's going to be a long winter," he said, shaking his head.

He made his way out of the mercantile, shivering at the icy blast of wind that caught him in the market square. It would be dark soon, and pulling up the collar of his overcoat, he hurried towards home. He did not take the direct route toward his *mamm's* house. That way would pass the home of Christian Schwartz, whose daughter, Sally, Paul had been engaged to earlier that year. But Sally had broken off the engagement, leaving Paul feeling devastated. She had taken up with another man, and he had heard they were to be married in the new year. He was trying not to let it bother him, as he could not help but feel a sense of upset and betrayal over what had happened. Try as he might, he could not lay the matter to rest, and it had been playing ever more heavily on his mind.

I just don't understand what I did to make her feel like that, he thought to himself, as he tramped through the snow.

Paul had been a devoted suitor. He had done everything for Sally and had even put a deposit down on a house for them to rent once they were married. It had all been planned, but Sally had changed her mind. He remembered the day it had happened. He had gone to her house with a bunch of roses to surprise her, only to find her talking to the man – Edward Moskar – at the gate. They had looked embarrassed but had made no attempt to hide their intentions, and Paul felt humiliated.

It still sickened his stomach to think of it. Try as he might, he could not rid himself of that dreadful image. It haunted him morning, noon, and night. His *mamm* lived at the top of a hill overlooking the market square. It was a trudge to the top, and Paul was slipping on the snow. He was approaching the gate, with its broken fence he had promised to mend when a familiar figure came in sight. It was Sarah Beiler, stopping to greet him as they passed.

"I've not seen you in weeks, Paul. How're you?" she asked.

Paul shook his head. He liked the Bishop's *fraa*. She always had time for everyone, and she had been a great support in the aftermath of his breakup with Sally.

"I'm not doing well, if I'm honest. I don't go out much. I just feel... so humiliated," he said, and Sarah patted him on the arm.

"You've nothing to be ashamed of, Paul. You don't need to hide yourself away like this. We all want to see you," she said.

Paul gave a weak smile. He knew he had done nothing wrong – nothing to deserve the treatment he had imposed on himself. Sympathy was with him, and Sally had found herself the object of gossip. But Paul could not feel any anger toward her. He simply felt sad at the loss of the happiness he had believed would be his for the rest of his life. He had loved Sally, and she had taken that love away from him.

"I know... it's just difficult, that's all," he said, lowering his head.

"Well... it's nearly Christmas. A time for new beginnings, don't you think? How's the nativity set coming along?" she asked.

Bishop Beiler had asked Paul to make a nativity set for the Christmas pageant. The figures from the old one had become worn and chipped, and their costumes were faded and frayed. Paul had been working hard on the figures, and the quilting circle, of which his *mamm* was a recent member, was to make the costumes. At the mention of the nativity set, Paul smiled. He was enjoying the work – it distracted him from his thoughts, and he was only too pleased to be doing something for the community.

"Oh, it's nearly finished. I've just got Mary to finish. The other figures are done, and then the quilting circle can dress them," he said.

"We've already started on some of the costumes," Sarah Beiler replied.

They exchanged a few further pleasantries and wished one another goodnight as the first flakes of a fresh snowfall could be felt in the air. Paul hurried through the gate and up onto the porch. His *mamm* had left a lamp burning in the window, and the smell of cooking hit him as he opened the door into the parlor. His *mamm* was there, sitting in a rocking chair by the stove. She was embroidering a lavish-looking hat, destined for one of the three kings, and she looked up at him and smiled.

"Am I getting a new fence for Christmas?" she asked.

Paul laughed. "*Jah, Mamm,* you're getting your new fence. But I've got to finish the nativity figures first. I don't want to let Bishop Beiler down," he said.

She smiled at him. "You won't, Paul. But you're late getting back, aren't you? I thought you only went to the mercantile," she said.

Paul recounted the story of the young woman who was repairing a chicken coop and his encounter with Sarah Beiler. His *mamm* laughed to hear the description of the woman in the mercantile.

"It sounds like she needs a carpenter, too. But don't go getting any ideas – nativity figures, then my fence. After that, you can repair as many chicken coops as you like," she said, getting to her feet and going into the kitchen to finish preparing their dinner.

Paul smiled to himself. It had not occurred to him to offer to help her in that way, nor had it occurred to him to even ask her name.

I should've asked her name. I should've told her mine. I could repair a chicken coop in my sleep, he thought to himself, feeling foolish for not having suggested he do so.

They ate a simple meal of buttered noodles and pork chops that evening. But as he went to bed, Paul could not help but dwell on thoughts of the woman he had encountered at the mercantile. She was very pretty, and there was a naivety about her he had found endearing, even as he admired her for rolling up her sleeves and attempting something most women would not dare to do.

"Perhaps I'll meet her again," he told himself, and it felt good to think of someone other than Sally.

His *mamm* had often told him to move on and stop dwelling in the past. But Paul had not been able to let go of those memories, nor the thought of his own inadequacies. But helping the woman in the mercantile had made him feel *gut*, and it was a feeling he wanted to experience again.

I'll try to find her, he vowed to himself, as he settled down to sleep that night, even allowing himself the thought of what might be if he pursued such an encounter further.

CHAPTER FOUR

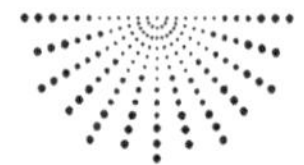

"Oh, no, not again," Miriam exclaimed, as the piece of wood she had so carefully balanced on one end of the chicken coop fell off.

She was attempting to nail one side at a right angle to the next. But as soon as she struck the wood, the frame gave way, and the other side fell. This was her fifth attempt, and she was growing increasingly frustrated.

It always looks so easy when men do it, she thought to herself, stepping back to admire her handiwork – an admiration that did not stretch very far.

The pieces of wood were just the right length, and the nails were the right size to go through the planks. But it was like a jigsaw without a picture, and Miriam was finding the task far harder than she had imagined. But pride prevented her from seeking help. She knew her *daed* would know just how to do it. But these were Miriam's hens, and Miriam wanted to be the one to build the coop for them. She balanced another piece of wood on the frame and was about to drive a nail through it when a voice behind her called out.

"Miriam, what're you doing out here in the snow? Come inside, we'll have coffee. I've brought a lemon cake," Barbara called out.

Miriam almost struck her finger with the hammer, and she turned to find her sister standing on the garden path, wrapped in a cloak, and wearing a headscarf over her *kapp*.

"I'm finishing the repairs to the coop," she replied.

Her sister rolled her eyes. "Get *daed* to do it. Come on, I want to get warm. My feet are like blocks of ice," she said.

Miriam knew Barbara would not take no for an answer, and reluctantly, she rose to her feet and followed her sister inside. Their *mamm* and *daed* were at the market, and Miriam put a kettle of water to boil on the stove, as Barbara cut thick slices of the cake for them to eat.

"Are Elijah and the twins all right?" Miriam asked as the two sisters sat down opposite one another by the stove with their coffee and cake a few moments later.

"Oh, yes, they're fine. They're looking forward to Christmas. It's not an easy time of year – but so much has changed since last Christmas. They talk about their *mamm* a lot more, and I think that's the best thing. It's like she's still part of the family. It's going to be a happy Christmas. We're all coming here, aren't we?" she said, and Miriam nodded.

She and her *mamm* had been busy with the preparations, and the house was already festooned with decorations.

"I'm so looking forward to it," Miriam replied.

"But still determined to raise a flock of chickens. What were you doing out there in the snow?" Barbara asked, shaking her head, and rolling her eyes.

Miriam felt embarrassed. She knew her sister thought her quite mad for her seeming obsession with the chickens. But taking care of her flock had given Miriam something to do in the months since Barbara's wedding, even as she knew it could not last forever.

"I was trying to repair the coop for the hens. They'll be much safer in there than in the shed," she replied.

Her sister looked skeptical.

"Not if it falls down on them, they won't," she replied.

"I'm trying my best. I... well, it's not easy," she said, and Barbara smiled.

"You need more than just a flock of chickens, Miriam. You need something to keep you occupied. A proper job. You can't just sell eggs at the market for the rest of your life," her sister replied.

Miriam felt deflated. Acquiring the chickens was supposed to give some purpose to her life, and whilst she had certainly found interest in her new hobby, she knew her sister was right. She could not remain a spinster forever, and even though her parents would never force the matter, Miriam knew she could not live forever on their charity.

"But it's a start, isn't it? I'm trying," she replied.

Barbara reached out and took her hand in hers. "I know you are. And I've not always been as grateful to you as I should've been. You looked after me so well during my convalescence, Miriam. You'd make a wonderful nurse. I will never forget what you did for me."

Miriam *had* enjoyed taking care of her sister, and the thought of becoming a nurse *had* crossed her mind. But she knew nothing of the process, or how she might go about it. Even as the seed was planted, she thought of a dozen reasons why it would not be possible.

"But looking after your sister isn't quite the same as taking care of patients in a hospital," she replied.

Barbara laughed. "You wouldn't be able to give them quite the attention you gave me – I couldn't move without my cushion being plumped or another cup of coffee offered. But seriously, Miriam, you've got a heart of gold, and anyone would be glad to have you taking care of them," she said.

Miriam smiled. It *was* a nice idea, even as she wondered as to the possibility of ever realizing it.

"I'd need some experience first, though. I suppose there're nursing colleges and so forth, but I couldn't pursue that without some experience," she said.

"And that's where I come in. I've had an idea," Barbara replied.

Miriam looked at her in surprise. She had not expected this. "What sort of idea?" she asked.

"Well, Susanna has a friend at the quilting circle. Her name's Sylvia Abrams. She needs some help around the house. Not nursing, exactly, but housekeeping. She needs someone to make meals for her and tidy up. She's got a son who lives with her, but he's out at work during the day and she's finding it harder to manage without him. What do you think?" Barbara asked.

Miriam thought for a moment. She knew she needed something other than chickens to occupy her time and working as a housekeeper would surely be *gut* experience if she decided to pursue the idea of nursing. She felt grateful to her sister for the suggestion, even as she had teased her for overbearingness during Barbara's convalescence.

"All right, I'll do it – if she wants me to, that is," Miriam replied.

Barbara smiled. "Oh, I'm so glad to hear you say that. She'll be so pleased. We can go up there tomorrow. She lives on the hill overlooking the market square. It's not far. I'll ask Susanna to come. She can make the introductions," Barbara replied, and the matter was settled.

Miriam took a second look at her sister, was there something more in that smile? *Nee,* she shook the idea off, she was just being silly. She felt a touch of excitement, was this a new beginning for her?

CHAPTER FIVE

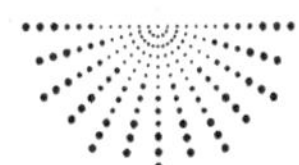

The next morning, Miriam found herself accompanying her sister and Susanna Bontrager – Barbara's *mamm*-in-law – through the snow towards the home of Sylvia Abrams.

Susanna had told Miriam more about the woman she was going to meet – she had recently joined the quilting circle and had been a widow for over twenty years. She had one son, Paul, who was often out at work, and usually spent her days alone.

It was Sarah Beiler who had suggested she join the quilting circle, and Susanna was going to take Sylvia to the home of Anna Troyer that very morning for a meeting of the circle.

"We're making costumes for the new nativity figures. It's Sylvia's son who's making them," Susann said, as they trudged up the hill toward Sylvia's house.

It was an attractive dwelling – large, and with a porch on two sides. The garden, too, was large, and Miriam noticed the fence had blown down and was in a state of some disrepair.

"I just hope I can help her," Miriam said, and Susanna smiled.

"She'll be grateful. But she was wary of trusting someone she didn't know. That's why she asked me if I knew anyone. She wanted a recommendation. I mentioned it to Barbara, and she immediately thought of you," Susanna replied.

They made their way across the garden and up the porch steps. The snow had drifted and was lying in banks across the garden. From the porch, Miriam could see across the whole of Faith's Creek, the landscape blanketed with snow, broken only by the occasional distant farm. It was so pretty and she took a moment to be grateful for all she had.

The door opened, and an elderly-looking woman with gray hair peeking out from her *kapp*, and hazel-colored eyes looked out at them.

"Good morning, Sylvia. I'd like you to meet someone. This is Miriam, my daughter-in-law's sister. I think she'd be the perfect match as a housekeeper for you," Susanna said.

Sylvia beamed at Miriam and breathed a sigh of relief.

"Oh, you're an answer to my prayers. You really are. I was just struggling with wood for the stove. Paul's out at work, and I don't like to trouble him with doing things around the house. If you can help me, it'd just be some cooking, housework, fetching and carrying, that sort of thing. I'd pay you by the hour and you could come and go as you wanted. Won't you come in?" she asked, standing aside with a look of delight on her face.

Miriam was surprised at the pace with which the interview had been conducted, but it seemed Sylvia trusted Susanna, and because Susanna trusted Barbara, and Barbara trusted Miriam, the matter could easily be settled. The house was comfortably furnished, and Sylvia pointed out with pride several pieces her son had made.

"You've got a lovely home, Sylvia," Susanna said.

Sylvia smiled. "My husband built it forty years ago, just after we were married. I couldn't imagine living anywhere else. But it's got too big for us, really. Having some help around the place is going to make such a difference to me," she said, smiling at Miriam.

That smile filled Miriam with joy, she was only too glad to have a purpose to fulfill.

They discussed several further particulars, and the arrangements were made. Miriam would go in every other day. She would prepare meals and clean and dust the parlor. Once a week, she would do the laundry, change the beds, and clean the bathroom. But it was companionship Sylvia wanted, too, and Miriam promised to sit and read to her, or simply sit and talk whenever her employer wished. She liked the idea of acting in such a way, and she was only too pleased to be asked to begin immediately.

"It'd be wonderful to come back from the quilting circle to the smell of something I haven't had to cook myself. You'll find plenty of things in the larder," Sylvia said, as she put on her shawl and checked her *kapp* in the mirror.

Miriam glanced at Barbara, who smiled and patted her arm.

"You'll be all right here, won't you, Miriam? We'll go off to the quilting circle now," she said.

Miriam nodded. "Is there anything particular you like to eat?" she asked, and Sylvia thought for a moment.

"Well... I do like buttered noodles. And Paul likes them, too. I always make buttered noodles on a Thursday, and today's Thursday so... why don't you make buttered noodles, and a casserole for tomorrow," she replied.

Miriam smiled, buttered noodles were easy and everyone loved them. "I can do that. It's no problem," she replied, feeling excited at the prospect of getting started.

The three women wished her goodbye, and Miriam was left alone in the house. She looked around her with interest, noticing the pieces of furniture made by Sylvia's son. They were fine pieces of craftsmanship. Miriam examined them with interest.

They're exquisite, she thought to herself, wishing she had a talent like that.

But she knew there were ways in which she could be useful, and she set about tidying the parlor, dusting the wooden surfaces, and setting the house in order. When she had finished, she looked around her with satisfaction and smiled at the thought of Sylvia returning to a tidy house. Now, she made her way into the kitchen and made herself familiar with where everything was. Buttered noodles were a specialty of her *mamm's,* and she intended to follow her recipe in the hope of pleasing her new employer. She found the ingredients easily enough and decided to make a chicken casserole for the following day, too, along with a batch of cinnamon cookies – another favorite of hers.

I think I'm going to really enjoy working for Sylvia, she thought to herself, as at last felt she had a purpose and a direction to follow.

CHAPTER SIX

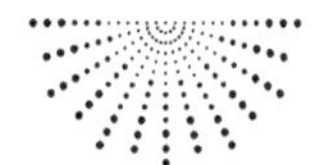

$\mathcal{P}$aul was concentrating hard. The faces were always the hardest part to craft. He had selected his smallest chisel and was making only the slightest movements across the wood – one false move and Mary's nose would be gone. He narrowed his eyes, squinting in the lamplight, before making a single stroke with the chisel, a slither of wood falling to the floor. He sat back with a sigh. He wanted the figures to be perfect, but he was growing tired, and darkness was never the friend of a woodworker.

"I'd better finish for the day," he told himself, glancing at the final nativity figure, whose face was still far from complete.

The others were finished and stood across the workshop awaiting the clothing promised by the quilting circle – Joseph, two shepherds, three kings, an innkeeper, the angel Gabriel, several assorted animals, and, of course, the infant Jesus himself. Paul had been working hard for the previous month, ever since Bishop Beiler had commissioned him to make new figures for the Faith's Creek nativity scene. The old ones had become chipped and roughed – they were no longer fitting for the celebration of Christmas – and Paul felt immensely proud at having been asked to create new figures for this year's pageant.

Was that a sin?

Nee, he didn't think *Gott* would mind.

The task had taken his mind off Sally and the sadness he had endured, and he would be sorry to finish the project, even as he would be glad to see the figures displayed.

I'm ready for something to eat, he thought to himself, as his stomach groaned while he swept up the wood chippings and set the workshop back in order.

He put on his overcoat and hat, wrapping a scarf around his neck against the chill air outside. He rented his workshop from one of the farmers – a lean-to building attached to a barn. He locked the door, padlocking it, and placing the key in his pocket. The walk home took him across the fields, and he trudged up the hill, rubbing his hands together against the cold. There was no lamp burning in the window. He recalled his *mamm* was out at the quilting circle, though a glow was coming from the kitchen window suggesting she had left a lamp burning there. He pulled off his boots on the porch and was surprised to find the door to the parlor open.

That's strange, he thought to himself, as he made his way inside.

A fire was kindled in the stove, and it seemed as though the parlor had been tidied, and everywhere dusted. A lamp burned on the table, and from the kitchen, a delicious smell was wafting.

Paul could hear humming, and curiously, he stepped forward, peering through the kitchen door. He was surprised to see a woman with her back to him. She was standing at the stove, and as he cleared his throat, she jumped and turned to look at him with a startled expression on her face. To his amazement, he recognized her – it was the same woman he had encountered in the mercantile store. The woman who was going to repair a chicken coop. What was she doing in his *mamm's* kitchen?

"Oh, I'm sorry. I didn't hear you come in," she exclaimed, looking terribly embarrassed.

Paul shook his head, still looking at her in confusion. "I don't understand – why are you here?" he asked.

The woman wiped her hands on a cloth and took off her apron looking worried, she nibbled her lip. "Oh... I thought you'd know. I suppose you wouldn't, though, would you? You weren't here this morning. I'm Miriam, Miriam Esch. I'm your *mamm's* new housekeeper," she said.

Paul vaguely recalled his *mamm* telling him she intended to get some help around the house. She had been struggling with the laundry, and whilst he had felt guilty at not being able to help out more, he had been so busy at work so as not to give the matter much thought.

"Oh, I didn't realize you were starting today," he said, as Miriam smiled and laughed.

"I didn't realize either. Well, not until this morning. It was my sister who suggested it. Your *mamm* had told Susanna Bontrager she needed some help – at the quilting circle. Susanna asked my sister, that's her daughter-in-law, and my sister suggested me," she replied.

Paul was not certain he entirely followed this line of reasoning, but he was grateful to Miriam for agreeing to help. The parlor was spotless, and the scent from the stove promised a fine dinner.

"That's very kind of you. She needed some help, and I'm out working all day. I can't do everything," Paul replied, once again remembering his promise to fix his *mamm's* fence.

"I've made buttered noodles for tonight, and a chicken casserole for tomorrow. I hope you'll like it," Miriam said.

Paul smiled. "I'm sure I will."

Just then, the door from the porch into the parlor opened, and his *mamm* appeared, rubbing her hands together against the cold.

"Oh, it's a bitter evening out there, isn't it?" she exclaimed, stomping the snow from her boots.

"How was the quilting circle?" Paul asked, going to help her with her overcoat.

"Oh, it was fine – but you know what women are like when they get together over coffee and cake. We finished quilting hours ago, and... oh, look at the parlor. Isn't it lovely and clean?" she said, looking around her and beaming.

Paul smiled. His *mamm* had always kept a pristine home, but arthritis was making it harder for her to see to the tasks she had once found easy, and lifting pots and pans in the kitchen, too, was becoming harder.

"I think we've got Miriam to thank for that," Paul replied, as Miriam appeared from the kitchen with a smile on her face.

"I'm so grateful to you, Miriam. I didn't expect you to do all this," Sylvia said, looking around her and shaking her head.

"I was glad to help. I hope I didn't do too much," Miriam replied.

Sylvia only laughed. "Too much? You've done more than you needed, but I appreciate it. Won't you stay for dinner? You cooked it after all."

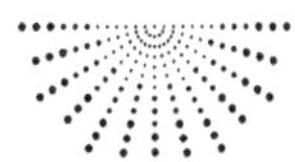

CHAPTER SEVEN

*M*iriam thanked her, and they sat down at the table, which had been neatly laid for them. A broth made from the carcass of the chicken cooked for tomorrow's casserole made a hearty starter, served with homemade bread, and it was followed by buttered noodles and pork chops, with sauerkraut and mustard.

Paul ate heartily, and he was glad to have Miriam join them. He had thought about her a lot since their encounter at the mercantile, and whilst he did not wish to embarrass her by asking about the chicken coop, he wondered what progress she had made on it.

"This is delicious, Miriam. Your *mamm's* taught you well, hasn't she?" Sylvia said as Miriam cleared the empty plates.

"I love cooking. Baking, especially. I'll make you a walnut cake when they're in season – or with some dried ones. I put coffee cream icing on it, too. It's my *daed's* favorite," Miriam replied, glancing at Paul, who smiled.

"Mine, too," he replied.

Paul was partial to a slice of cake – his favorite was his *mamm*'s seed cake, but coffee and walnut sounded delicious. Miriam had made stewed apples for dessert, and when the meal was finished, Paul felt thoroughly satisfied.

"Well, I've had a lovely day – quilting, chatting with my friends, and now a delicious dinner I didn't have to cook myself and a parlor as clean as a whistle," Sylvia said, rising from her chair and yawning.

"Why don't you sit in front of the stove, *Mamm*. I'll walk Miriam home," Paul said, even as Miriam began to protest.

"I'll see to the dishes first," she said, but Paul shook his head.

"It's getting late. I can wash a few plates, it's all right. That was a delicious dinner, *denke*. I insist on walking you home, though," he said.

Miriam smiled. "That's very kind of you," she replied and went to fetch her overcoat and scarf.

"I wish we'd met years ago, Miriam," Sylvia said, thanking her profusely once again.

"I'm pleased I could help you. Shall I come back tomorrow?" Miriam replied.

"Only if you want to. We've got the casserole, but... there's plenty we could do," Sylvia replied, and it was agreed Miriam would return the next day.

Paul was grateful to Miriam for her help. His *mamm* had been struggling, and he had been uncertain how to help her. He was no cook, and after work, all he wanted to do was rest. He put on his boots and overcoat, and the two of them stepped out onto the porch. It was snowing again, and Miriam shivered.

"We had cold winters in Idaho, but this is something else," she said, as they walked down the steps and across the garden.

"You only came to Faith's Creek recently?" Paul asked, and Miriam nodded.

She explained how her family had come from Idaho, but she had remained something of a recluse through no fault of her own. She had been taking care of her sister, Barbara, who was now married to Elijah Bontrager.

"I didn't have much to do after she was married," Miriam said, shaking her head.

"And that's why you started keeping chickens, is it?" Paul asked.

He had not yet raised the subject, but he could not pretend their encounter at the mercantile had not occurred. Miriam blushed and shook her head.

"Oh, the chickens... well, yes, I'm not sure I've had the greatest of successes. They lay for me, and I've only lost two to the fox. It's a lot harder than it looks, though," she said.

They were walking down the hill now, and Miriam was holding onto Paul's arm lest she slip. Sally's house lay just along the road – in the direction they needed to take unless they were to go the long way around. This was the point where Paul usually turned the other way, but Miriam would think him ridiculous if he did so, taking a deep breath, he proceeded on in the direction of the house she shared with her parents, passing Sally's porch a moment later. But he did not give the house a second glance – he would be glad if she saw him, for there was no shame in walking a woman home at night.

"And the chicken coop?" he asked.

Miriam paused and smiled.

"It's a work in progress," she replied.

They had reached her house now, and Paul could see over the hedge to where the dilapidated chicken coop stood. Miriam had made a valiant effort at repair, but one side was falling in, and the roof was half off. The planks of wood she had bought at the mercantile stood stacked up to the side, covered in the fresh snow. It looked a sorry sight.

"I can see you need a bit of help," he said, raising his eyebrows.

Miriam laughed and turned away in embarrassment.

"Well... perhaps a little," she replied.

"I'll help you fix it," Paul said.

He was not sure what had come over him. He had not yet fixed his *mamm*'s fence, and the nativity figures still had to be completed. But there was something about Miriam he found endearing – more than that, he found her charming and ever so pretty. He was grateful to her for helping his *mamm*, and as she wished him goodnight, he found himself looking forward to seeing her again.

"I'd be glad of your help," she replied, and he smiled at her.

"I'll make it a chicken coop fit for any hen who chooses to grace it," he replied, as he watched her hurry up the path.

She paused on the porch and waved to him, and as he returned home that evening, Paul could not help but wonder where this new found friendship would go...

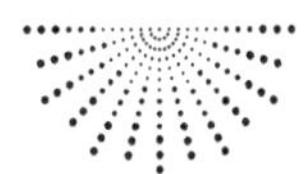

CHAPTER EIGHT

"I'm proud of you, Miriam. You'll be a real help to Sylvia, I know you will," Miriam's *mamm* said, as Miriam prepared to leave for work the next morning.

She was taking a box of eggs to Sylvia and had wrapped them and put them in a basket, along with a dozen bread rolls she had baked the previous evening.

"She's really nice. It doesn't feel like work. I ate with them last night, and Sylvia's going to be there today, too. I'm sure we'll have lots to talk about," she said, checking her *kapp* in the mirror. It was straight but it had a habit of slipping; she couldn't understand how other women kept it in place., Her *mamm* and sister made it look so effortless. Adjusting it, she smiled at her *mamm* and made her way from the house.

The snow clouds had cleared, leaving behind a bright, frosty morning. The chill made the air tingle in her lungs but she enjoyed it and looked forward to the walk.

Miriam made her way along the road and up the hill towards Sylvia's house, breathing in the fresh air, and wondering what the day would bring. As she reached the gate, she saw Paul on the porch, pulling on his boots. He smiled at her as she approached, rising to his feet and tipping an imaginary hat to her.

"*Gut* morning," he said.

Miriam smiled, pleased to see him. "It's a lovely morning," she replied.

"It is, I'll miss it as I'll be inside the workshop carving." He cocked his head. "I don't begrudge it, though, I love what I do." He stepped down from the porch.

"You're making the nativity figures, aren't you?" she asked, for her *mamm* had mentioned the costumes to her the evening before.

"That's right. I've just got Mary to finish," he replied, grinning at her.

"That's very important, so I won't keep you. It's not long until the pageant," Miriam replied.

She remembered the excitement of the previous year – how the whole of the community had turned out for the traditional start of the Christmas season in Faith's Creek. She was looking forward to seeing the nativity figures at the pageant and had already seen Mary's blue costume, thanks to her *mamm*, who was making it.

"I'll see you later – *Mamm's* very excited about you coming this morning. It's *gut* company for her," Paul said, and whistling to himself, he walked off along the snow-covered path and out of the gate.

Miriam knocked at the door, and Sylvia opened it with a beaming smile on her face. "You don't need to knock. Just come straight in," she said, stepping back and beckoning Miriam inside.

The stove had been lit, and the parlor felt cheerful against the chill of the outside. The house looked so cozy and Miriam put down her basket and smiled at Sylvia. With the door shut it felt even nicer and she could see that Sylvia was looking forward to her visit. Just like Paul, Miriam realized that she enjoyed her job too, how delightful was that!

"I thought we could clear out a few cupboards this morning. After forty years, this house needs a good sort out," Sylvia said.

"Ack, that is something we all could do more often. There are always those bits that get pushed to the back and forgotten. A jar here, a packet there." Miriam was only too pleased to help.

The two of them spent a happy morning tidying out cupboards in the kitchen and the dresser, before sitting down to a simple lunch of soup and bread.

"I bumped into Paul as I was leaving this morning. He said he only had one nativity figure to finish. It was Mary. My *mamm's* made her costume," Miriam said, suddenly realizing that she had worked up an appetite and the soup tasted all the better for it.

"He's been so focused on making the figures. I'm so proud of him. It's helped him a lot since Sally," Sylvia replied.

Miriam looked at her in confusion. She had not heard of Sally and wondered who she was. "Sally?" she asked.

A sorrowful look came over Sylvia's face. "Of course, you might not know. Sally Schwartz was the love of Paul's life. They were due to be married in the summer.

But she broke off the engagement and went chasing off after... oh, I can't even bring myself to mention his name. It broke Paul's heart. He's not been the same since," she said, sighing and shaking her head.

Miriam felt terribly sorry for Paul. He had surely been humiliated by Sally's actions, and it was no wonder he shut himself away in his workshop every day. "That's awful. Did she give a reason for breaking things off?" Sylvia asked.

"She wanted to marry that other man instead... he had better prospects... according to her. It was like she was choosing at the market. *Nee* thought of happiness, or loyalty, or all the things that money can't buy. I thought we were better than that, but there are still some that think status is worth more than love. Paul did everything for her. He doted on her. He was totally in love with her, but... well, sometimes things don't work out, do they?" Sylvia seemed to have lost a little of her light.

Miriam shook her head. "I'm so sorry." Of course, she was, though she really had no reference by which to agree or disagree. She had never been in love, nor had anyone been in love with her. She had not felt the pain of loss or separation. She had not had her own feelings rejected or rejected the feelings of another.

"And he hasn't thought about marrying since?" Miriam ventured, curious as to how Paul now viewed the possibility of another relationship.

"I don't know. I wish he would. He'd be so much happier if he let her go and moved on. It was not fair to him... but life isn't fair, I suppose," Sylvia replied.

Miriam nodded. She *did* know that, and there was much in her own life she considered unfair. She thought of Barbara – even as she felt guilty for doing so. She didn't resent her sister, but sometimes she was a little envious. Barbara had everything, or so it seemed. She was married, she had a family, and prospects for the future.

Once again, Miriam felt inadequate, even as she knew how hard she had worked since the day of Barbara and Elijah's wedding. She had her flock of chickens, she sold eggs at the market, she had made new friends, and now she had a job she was enjoying greatly. But try as she might, she could not help but compare herself to her sister, and in that comparison, she always fell short.

"I hope he'll find the happiness he deserves," Miriam said as she took the dirty dishes through to the kitchen to wash.

The two women spent the afternoon cleaning out more cupboards in the parlor. Miriam was amazed at the number of things Sylvia had collected over the years, and they were able to put aside several boxes of ornaments for the bric-à-brac fair to be held in aid of the pageant.

"I didn't realize I had all this stuff," Sylvia said, as she opened another cupboard and pulled out several more boxes to sort.

But as she did so, footsteps on the porch announced the return of Paul, and Miriam straightened up, brushing the dust from her dress as the door opened, and Sylvia's son appeared. He smiled at Miriam, closing the door behind him, and shivering.

"It's getting colder out there. We're due some more snow, I think," he said, as Sylvia, too, got up from the floor by the cupboard.

"We've been sorting bric-à-brac for the pageant fundraiser. I've got so many trinkets, they all need a *gut* clean, then we can raise some money with them," she said.

Paul smiled and shook his head. "When you get an idea into your head, *Mamm*, that's it. Have you had Miriam on her knees all day sorting out your cupboards?" he asked, sitting down on a chair next to the stove and holding out his hands to warm them.

"I don't mind," Miriam replied.

She had been pleased to help, and now she was looking forward to sharing dinner with them, and to Paul walking her home.

"She's relentless. She'll have you sorting the whole house out. Don't look in the box room – it's full from floor to ceiling," Paul replied, laughing as his *mamm* tried to appear put out, even as the corners of her mouth displayed a smile.

"And speaking of getting ideas in my head – when am I getting my fence fixed? What's the point of having a carpenter for a son if I don't get any carpentry done? You wouldn't like it if I got Joseph Flaud's boy to do it, would you?" she said, raising her eyebrows.

Paul laughed again.

"You know he doesn't do a *gut* job – that's why Bishop Beiler asked me to do the nativity figures. Jobadiah 'fixed' the bishop's roof, and it leaked worse than it did before," Paul replied.

Sylvia laughed. "*Ack*, that is true."

Miriam retreated to the kitchen at this point, and it was not long before she had dinner ready. She liked eating with Paul and Sylvia. The conversation flowed freely, and she learned a great deal about Faith's Creek and its history.

"We've lived in this community for six generations," Sylvia told her proudly, and there was much talk of the changes her family had seen.

After dinner, Paul offered to walk Miriam home, and she was only too glad to accept, even as she knew it meant him going back out into the cold.

"It's very kind of you to walk me home like this," Miriam said as she held onto his arm over a tricky patch of ice, and they made their way down the hill through the snow.

"Not at all. I'm happy to. You've really helped my *mamm*. I'm so grateful. I hope she's not expecting too much of you," he said.

Miriam shook her head.

She liked working for Sylvia, and it had been her decision to work that day.

"I like it. She's such a lovely person. I like being there. I just hope I'm not... overstepping the mark," she said.

Paul laughed. "Tidying the house? Making dinner? Keeping everything nice? You are doing a fabulous job and you seem to have brought some joy into the house," he replied.

Miriam felt a flush of heat rising up her face. She had worked hard, and it felt good to be congratulated for her efforts. They had reached her gate now, and she turned to Paul and smiled.

"I'm glad I could help. I'll call in tomorrow. I know it's Saturday, but your *mamm* could use the help. I think if I don't come she will do it all herself. Things are always busier in the run up to Christmas, aren't they?" she said.

Paul nodded, and he rummaged in his pocket and brought out a small parcel – brown paper wrapped around a small object. He looked a little embarrassed but handed it to her with a smile.

Miriam looked at it curiously. "What's this?" she asked.

"Open it," he said, and Miriam tore off the paper and opened the package.

Inside, delicately carved, was a Christmas ornament. It was a snowflake, each piece bound together with string. It was beautiful. She held it up to get a better look in the light from the moon, which had just appeared from behind a cloud.

"It's stunning," she exclaimed.

"I thought you could hang it in the window as a decoration," he said, sounding somewhat bashful as he spoke.

"*Denke, denke* so much."

"I wanted to offer you some help too," he said. "I would love to fix your chicken coop."

For a moment he saw a cloud pass over her eyes. Did she think that he judged her? "It is what I do for a living," he said. "I meant *nee* offense."

Miriam smiled. "None was taken, I just wish I was better at it."

"*Ack,* you have a way with people, I have a way with wood but am terrible with people. We all have our path."

Miriam felt those words touch her deeply, he was right, she was judging herself against others and that was not necessary, it was not the way that *Gott* would judge her, He would judge her by what was in her heart.

But Miriam held the exquisite snowflake and felt filled with joy that he would help her. "I would like that very much," she said, and without thinking, she reached up and kissed him on the cheek.

"It's lovely, *denke*," she said, and wishing him goodnight, she hurried up the path, turning to wave to him from the porch.

Inside, her *mamm* and *daed* were sitting by the stove. Miriam went at once to hang the wooden snowflake in the window.

"What's that, Miriam?" her *mamm* asked, looking up at her with a smile.

"It's a snowflake, Paul made it for me," she replied, as she stood back to admire the beautiful carving. It was painted silver and seemed to glisten in the lamplight. Miriam could not help but wonder if that snowflake brought with it something more...

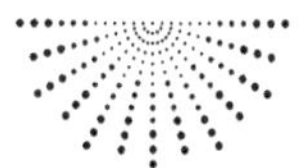

"That's how I want it, just like that," Paul exclaimed, rising to his feet and stepping back to look down at the face of Mary – the final figure in the nativity scene.

He had been working hard all day, and whilst the face had previously eluded him, Paul had eventually found inspiration from Miriam. He had modeled the *mamm* of Jesus on her, and the face of the virgin looked very beautiful.

Paul was a skilled craftsman, and he had carved the figure to appear as though it were looking down at the sleeping infant. He was pleased with his work, and rose to his feet, dusting off the wood chippings from his apron and stretching out his arms.

"And just in time, too," he said to himself.

The day of the pageant was fast approaching, and the nativity figures would need to be set up in the barn behind the schoolhouse where the performance was to take place. His *mamm* had told him the costumes were ready, and all that was needed now was to dress the figures and lay out the scene. Paul could not wait to see the final display, and he felt certain the people of Faith's Creek would be gladdened by the sight. It was a reminder of the true meaning of Christmas and it made him feel both small and insignificant, and yet, meaningful and loved. He had finished early and was looking forward to arriving home and putting his feet up. But there was another reason Paul wanted to get home early – Miriam.

He had thought a lot about her in recent days, and he had enjoyed walking her home each evening after dinner. It had become something of a ritual for them, something he looked forward to. He had still not fixed her chicken coop. Also, he needed to find the time to fix his *mamm's* fence – but he had promised Miriam he would see to it before Christmas. The snowflake had been happily received, and Paul had been pleased to see it hanging in the window of Miriam's house as he had passed that way earlier in the day. He put on his overcoat and scarf, casting a final look at the nativity figures, his eyes falling on Mary, whose face so well resembled that of Miriam.

I'm proud of what I've done, he thought to himself, as he felt at last as though he were breaking free of Sally's hold over him.

He had spent so long in the depths of despair, but meeting Miriam had changed that, and Paul was beginning to wonder if he might have a future after all. It made him happy to think this way, and even the thick snow and chilly air could not dampen his spirits.

"I'm home, *Mamm,*" he called out, as he entered the house a short while later.

A delicious smell was coming from the kitchen, and Paul hoped to see Miriam's smiling face appear. But it was his *mamm* who called out a greeting from upstairs, and a moment later, she appeared, smiling at him as she came downstairs.

"Oh, you're back early," she said.

Paul nodded. "I've finished the figures now," Paul said, glancing around for Miriam.

"That's *gut*. We'll get the costumes on them tomorrow, then we can set up the nativity scene. I can't wait to see it all come together. You've worked so hard, Paul. I'm proud of you," she said, patting his arm.

Paul was still hoping to see Miriam, and it seemed his *mamm* had realized that too, as now she turned to him with a smile.

"Is... Miriam not here?" he asked.

"I sent her home early. Her *mamm* has a sore throat. I told her I could manage here," Sylvia replied.

Paul's face fell. "Oh... will she be here tomorrow?" he asked.

"She will, *jah*." Sylvia shook her head and laughed.

"What's the matter?" Paul asked.

"You're the matter. You've fallen for her, haven't you?"

Paul blushed. He had not realized it was that obvious. His feelings for Miriam were confused, or rather, his feelings about what was right for him were confused. He had vowed never to trust another woman as long as he lived. Sally had broken his heart, but he knew he had tarred all women with the memory of what she had done to him. Not all women were like Sally – Miriam had begun to prove that to him, even as he was uncertain of whether to pursue those feelings further. He did not want to get hurt again, and the thought of being so was enough to hold him back.

"Well... I like her. She's so sweet and kind. She'd done so much for you, and the house is so..." he began, but his *mamm* rolled her eyes and interrupted.

"Oh, Paul, it doesn't matter what she's done for me. It matters how you feel about her. She's a lovely person. She's bright, kind, and caring. She's just the sort of woman you need," she said.

Paul smiled. His *mamm* never held back on her opinions. She had been forthright about Sally – critical of her, even when Paul had been blinkered as to the truth.

"I know, *Mamm*. But I... I don't know. Maybe I should pursue it. We've been getting to know one another and I enjoy her company." What he didn't say was how much he looked forward to it. "I promised to fix her chicken coop," he said, knowing what his *mamm* would say to that.

"Then you'd better get on with it. You're not going to impress her by delaying her repairs for as long as you've delayed my fence," she said with a wink.

Paul laughed. "I promised I'd do the fence, didn't I? And I promised I'd mend the chicken coop, too. It's just… after Sally, I don't want to be hurt again," he said, shaking his head.

Try as he might, Paul could not rid himself of the possibility of a broken heart. He had felt just like this about Sally. He had fallen in love with her too quickly and had paid the price for such haste. If he was to pursue a relationship with Miriam, he wanted to make sure it was right.

"Mend the coop. Take a risk. Show her you've got feelings for her. I think you might be surprised," Sylvia said.

Paul nodded. "I'll think about it," he replied, sitting down by the stove with a sigh.

CHAPTER TEN

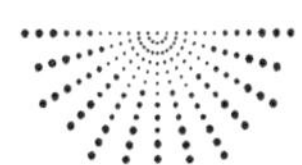

"You're running a bit of a temperature, *Mamm*," Miriam said, as she removed the thermometer from her *mamm's* mouth and held it up to the lamplight.

"Oh... I can't get ill at this time of year. There's too much to do," Lavinia managed, before descending into a bout of coughing.

Miriam looked at her sympathetically. Her *mamm's* symptoms were getting worse, and she wondered whether to go out in the snow and fetch Doctor Yoder.

"I'll get another blanket and bring you another cup of chicken soup," Miriam replied.

Her *mamm* gave a weak smile. "I'll say it again, Miriam – your sister's right, you'd make a wonderful nurse," she said.

Miriam smiled, she liked the idea, caring for Sylvia had brought such joy to her life. She went upstairs to fetch another blanket. Darkness had fallen, and the weather was coming in – the wind had picked up, and the windows were rattling, as snow drove against them.

What an awful night, she thought to herself, opening a cupboard and taking out a blanket.

As she did so, she glanced out of the window. She could see the chicken shed, the door of which had blown open and was swinging back and forth with such ferocity, Miriam feared it would come off. She hurried back downstairs, gave her *mamm* the blanket, and went to pull on her outdoor shoes and overcoat.

"Goodness me, where are you going, Miriam? Can't you hear the weather out there," her *daed* said.

"The door to the hen shed – it's blown open. I don't want the snow getting in there. They'll freeze," she replied, and without waiting for her *daed* to object, Miriam hurried out into the night.

The wind was howling, and the snow was drifting in great banks across the garden. Miriam had to steady herself, fearing she would be knocked off her feet. She made her way around the side of the house to where the shed stood, the door banging ever more loudly as the wind kept catching it. Miriam ran across the garden, taking hold of the shed door and pulling it closed. She drove the bolt across, sighing with relief at not having found the chickens wandering around the garden. They would have been blown away for certain.

"There now, that's better," she told herself, anxious to get back inside.

She turned and made her way across the garden. A gust of wind almost knocked her off her feet, and as she tried to stand up, a creaking noise came from the dilapidated chicken coop. Suddenly, a piece of wood was ripped clean away from it, and the wind tossed it toward Miriam, knocking her to the ground. She screamed, calling out for help as she lay dazed in the snow. Struggling to get up, she called out again.

"Help, *Daed*, help me, please," she cried, as the wind whipped the snow around her, and her whole body felt chilled to the bone. A wave of dizziness went over her and she felt her eyes beginning to close.

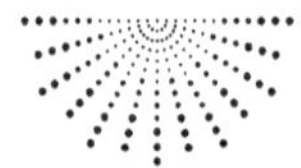

"**I** just don't know where she is. She said she'd be here first thing," Sylvia said, peering out of the parlor window.

Paul was eating breakfast at the table, and he took a sip of coffee, before replying.

"Wasn't her *mamm* sick yesterday? Perhaps she's had to stay with her. Or perhaps she's got it herself. She wouldn't want to come if it's catching," he replied.

"*Nee...* but, I'm worried about her. I'll walk down there and see," Sylvia replied.

"*Mamm*, why don't you wait for half an hour. I'll come with you... if you want me to?" Paul said.

She turned to him and nodded. She looked worried, even though Paul did not think there was anything to worry about. He finished his breakfast and helped her clear up. They were just putting away the plates when a knock came at the door.

"Oh, thank goodness, that'll be her now, won't it?" Sylvia said, wiping her hands on a cloth and hurrying to open the door.

But it was not Miriam who stood on the porch, and as Paul emerged from the kitchen, he saw Susanna Bontrager with an anxious expression on her face.

"Sylvia, thank goodness you're in. There's been a terrible accident," she said, as Sylvia ushered her inside.

"What's happened?" Sylvia asked, a hand on her chest.

She closed the door, and Susanna shook her head, sighing as she sat down on the chair she was now offered.

"Last night... it's Miriam. She went out to close the chicken shed up. The wind was so terrible – it tore off a piece of that dilapidated old chicken coop she's been fixing up. The piece of wood hit her squarely on the head. She's got a concussion, and she got cold out there, too. It was her *daed* who found her. Doctor Yoder's been to see her too. But I knew you'd be worried if she didn't turn up," Susanna replied.

Paul was horrified, and he shook his head in disbelief, even as a terrible thought occurred to him. He had promised to repair the chicken coop. If he had done so, the piece of wood would not have broken off. The accident was his fault...

"Is she... all right?" he asked, even though he knew it was a foolish question.

Susanna shook her head. "She's in bed now. She's got a nasty bump to the head. It's going to take a few days before she's feeling any better. I just thought you should know. She won't be working for a while," Susanna replied.

Sylvia shook her head, glancing at Paul as she did so.

"Oh, that doesn't matter. All that matters is her getting better. It's too awful, the poor dear. I must visit her."

"I'm going back down there now. You could come, too. She'd be pleased to see you, I'm sure," Susanna said.

This statement was directed at Paul's *mamm*, even as Paul felt desperately guilty at having caused the accident. He should have repaired the chicken coop – there had been ample opportunity to do so.

"I'll come, gladly, I will. I'll take her some of the butter cookies she baked yesterday. They're delicious. I'm sure they'll make her feel better," Sylvia said, and she was soon bundled up against the cold, and following Susanna out of the house.

"Give Miriam my best wishes," Paul said.

His *mamm* turned to him and nodded, the worry clear on her face. "I will. I'm sure she'll be all right," she said, oblivious, it seemed, to Paul's sense of guilt.

As the door closed behind them, he sighed and sank down into a chair, putting his head into his hands,

"Why didn't I just repair it?" he asked himself, even as he knew it was too late now.

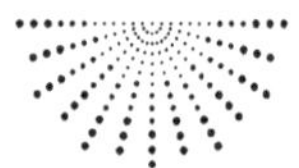

CHAPTER TWELVE

Miriam was sitting up in bed. Her head ached terribly, and she felt dizzy and confused. She could not remember much about the accident, except she had been struck by a piece of wood, and later found herself in bed. It had been her *daed* who had found her, and now he was standing at her bedside, looking anxiously down at her.

"How're you feeling this morning? Did you sleep?" he asked as her *mamm* bustled into her bedroom with a tray.

"I've made you some porridge, and there's sweet tea and rolls with butter and jam," she said, setting the tray down on the bedside table and looking at Miriam with an anxious expression on her face.

"You... you shouldn't be doing that, *Mamm*. You're not well," Miriam said, but her *mamm* shook her head.

"It's only a slight temperature, that's all. It's you I'm worried about. Doctor Yoder said you've had a nasty bump on the head," she said.

Miriam raised her hand to her head. The bandage was wrapped around her forehead, and the wound beneath felt tender to the touch.

"It feels like it... I don't remember much of what happened. But it was the hen coop, wasn't it?" she said.

Her *daed* nodded. "A piece of wood came off it in the wind. It was a freak accident. I heard you call out for help and came running. I found you on your back in the snow. You were in a sorry state, Miriam," he said, shaking his head.

"I'm glad you found me. I don't know... it doesn't bear thinking about. But I'll be all right, won't I?" Miriam asked.

Her *mamm* sat on the edge of the bed and patted her hand. "You'll be fine. But you need to rest," she said, as the sound of a knock at the door came from below.

Lavinia went to answer it, and her *daed* leaned down to put his arms around her. He was not a man who often gave in to emotion, but Miriam could tell he was upset.

"I'm sorry, Miriam. I shouldn't have let you go out in the snow on your own. I should've come with you," he said.

Miriam shook her head and smiled at him as he straightened up. "You couldn't have known what was going to happen. I rushed out when I saw the shed door blowing open. It was just... an accident," she said, as her *daed* brushed a tear from his eyes.

He was about to reply, but a clattering on the stairs brought visitors. It was Barbara, accompanied by Susanna, Sarah Beiler, Sylvia, and Anna Troyer. Miriam smiled at them, as a collective expression of sympathy came into the room.

"You poor thing, how terrible," Anna exclaimed.

"Is it hurting a lot?" Barbara asked, and the others expressed similar sentiments.

Miriam was presented with several dozen cookies, a basket of fruit, and a seed cake, all of which came with *gut* wishes for a swift recovery.

"I'm feeling a little better," Miriam said, as the women crowded around her bed.

"I was so worried when Susanna came to tell me. Don't you worry about work. I can manage," Sylvia said.

"It's very kind of you all to come," she said, and the women smiled at her.

"Not at all. You're part of the family," Anna said.

Miriam smiled. "You mean the quilting circle? I'm not much of a quilter, though," she said, but the women shook their heads.

"Your *mamm's* been one of our staunchest members since you all arrived in Faith's Creek. And now you're working for Sylvia, too – that makes it official," Anna replied, and the others nodded.

Miriam smiled. She was truly grateful to the quilting circle for their kindness, even as she was unsure she deserved it.

"Between us, I think Paul felt a little guilty this morning when he heard the news. He didn't say anything, and I didn't say anything, either," Sylvia said.

Miriam looked at her curiously.

There was no reason why Paul should feel guilty. It had nothing to do with him, and she was only sorry she would not see him in the coming days or be able to attend the pageant and see the unveiling of the nativity scene.

"Guilty? Why should he feel guilty? It was me who went out in that awful weather," Miriam replied, looking confused.

Her head was still hurting, and the voices of her visitors were making it worse. She wanted to rest, even as she was trying to be polite.

"Because he didn't mend your chicken coop, that's why," Sylvia replied.

Miriam laughed. "I should've made sure it was secure myself," she said, for there was no reason to blame Paul for an accident she had caused herself.

The chicken coop had been a disaster, and it had been kind of Paul to offer to repair it in the first place. There was no blame in that, and Miriam would not hear of Paul feeling guilty.

"It was just the look he had on his face. I'll be sure to tell him you're getting better," Sylvia replied.

"The two of you get on well, don't you?" Susanna said, and the women exchanged glances.

Miriam nodded, even as she yawned and closed her eyes for a moment.

"We do, yes," she said.

"We should leave you to rest. We'll call again in a few days. We can tell you all about the pageant," Sarah Beiler said, and the women wished Miriam goodbye.

"Wasn't that kind of them?" her *mamm* said when she returned from seeing their guests out.

"It was very kind, yes," Miriam replied, but she could not help but dwell on the strange revelation of Paul's self-imposed guilt.

He had no reason to feel guilty, and Miriam hoped he would soon realize there was no blame on his part, even as she hoped her next visitor might be him...

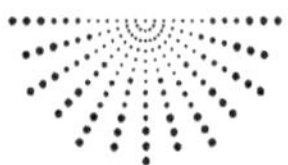

CHAPTER THIRTEEN

"I'm telling you, Paul. She doesn't blame you for anything," Sylvia said, rolling her eyes.

But Paul was not convinced. It was the day of the pageant, and he was busy putting the finishing touches to the figures for the nativity scene. But his thoughts were elsewhere, and he found himself preoccupied with his feelings of guilt over Miriam's accident.

It had been two days since Susanna Bontrager had delivered the devastating news, and Paul had hardly dared to believe what his *mamm* had told him. There was no doubt in his mind that Miriam blamed him for the accident. He had made a promise, and that promise had been broken, resulting in a terrible tragedy. He had not plucked up the courage to visit

Miriam, even as his *mamm* had encouraged him to do so.

"But... I was supposed to fix the chicken coop, wasn't I? If I'd done that, she'd be all right," he exclaimed.

Sylvia shook her head. "And if you'd fixed my fence, would that have solved any problems? Accidents happen. We can't blame one thing on another. We'd go all the way back to *Gott* if we did that – and there's plenty who blame *Gott* for things that are their fault entirely. Miriam doesn't blame you, Paul. She thinks the world of you," Sylvia replied.

Paul was not convinced. He had tried his best to convince himself otherwise, but try as he might, he still could not get the thought of his own responsibility out of his head.

"I just feel... I should've done something more," he said.

Sylvia shook her head. "She'll get better, Paul. Don't make yourself miserable over it. Why don't you go and see her?" she asked.

Paul had thought a great deal about the possibility of visiting Miriam, even as he had dreaded the thought, too. He did not know if he could face her. His *mamm* had told him she did not blame him in any way for the accident, but she was so kind and generous, he wondered if really, she was harboring a great deal of hurt.

"Perhaps after the pageant," he said.

Sylvia rolled her eyes. "Well, we'd better get ready for the pageant, hadn't we?"

Paul nodded. His mind was still elsewhere, but he knew he had a job to do, and Bishop Beiler and the rest of the community were relying on him. He had enlisted the help of several friends – including Fletch, the mercantile store clerk – to help him. They arrived a few moments later, and the figures – which had been brought to the house the previous evening for dressing – were loaded onto a wagon, drawn by a large shire horse.

"It's impressive, that's for certain," Fletch said, as he followed Paul at the side of the wagon, which was being driven by another of their friends.

"I just hope Bishop Beiler likes them," Paul replied.

He was doubting himself now – not just over Miriam's accident, but everything else, too. Would the figures really be a fitting display for the start of the Christmas season? He knew how important the nativity scene was to the people of Faith's Creek, and he wanted everything to be perfect. The pageant was to be held in the barn behind the schoolhouse, and as they arrived, Amanda Bride, one of the nursery school teachers, and the organizer of the yearly pageant came to greet them.

"I'm so excited to see the figures," she said, as Paul and the others began to unload them from the cart.

They were covered in blankets to protect them from the weather, and they had brought bundles of straw to set out for a stable.

"I just hope everyone likes them," Paul replied, still doubting himself terribly, even as Amanda assured him they would be perfect.

"Come on inside, we've just got time to set them up before people start arriving," she said, leading them inside.

Several dozen *kinner* were practicing a song on the stage for the pageant, and the area where the nativity scene was to be set up had been cleared and made ready. Paul directed where the figures should be placed, though the blankets remained, until the straw, too, had been arranged.

Paul was meticulous in his preparations, and the figures looked far bigger than they had done in his workshop. Just as they were finishing, Bishop Amos Beiler and his *fraa*, Sarah, arrived. He greeted Paul warmly, and Paul felt suddenly very nervous about the unveiling. He would be the center of attention – something he had avoided astutely since his breakup with Sally.

"I can't wait to see them," Amos said, as Paul arranged the last of the straw.

"Do you want to unveil them after the performance?" Paul asked, and the Bishop nodded.

"We'll let the *kinner* have their moment, then we'll see the figures," he replied.

The barn was beginning to fill with the audience – parents of the *kinner*, members of the community, and younger siblings not yet old enough to take part. It was quite a crowd, and amongst them, Paul spotted Barbara and Elijah, who had come to watch Elijah's twins in the performance. His own *mamm* had come, too, and she came to join him at the side by the nativity scene.

"How're you feeling?" she asked.

"Nervous," Paul admitted.

He kept glancing over toward Barbara, wondering if she, too, blamed him for the accident. But at that moment, Bishop Beiler called for attention – the pageant was about to begin. In their own inimitable way, the *kinner* of Faith's Creek told the story of the first Christmas.

They had been practicing for weeks, and when the finale came, there was not a dry eye in the barn. Everyone applauded, and the *kinner* took a bow, as Bishop Beiler climbed onto the stage to thank Amanda and the *kinner* for all their hard work.

"I think we can all agree this is the start of Christmas in Faith's Creek. To hear the Christmas story told, and to be reminded afresh of what it means. But we've another hallowed tradition in Faith's Creek – the nativity scene – but this year, we've got a new one," he said, turning to Paul, who nodded shyly.

"I'm only too glad to have been asked to make the figures. They're a little bigger than the previous ones. But I hope everyone's going to like them. They're not entirely my own work, the quilting circle – led by Anna Troyer – made the costumes, and I'm grateful to Fletch and some of the other mercantile store clerks for helping me cut the wood and move figures. I'd like to thank Bishop Beiler, too, for putting his trust in me," he said, his heart beating fast as Fletch and the others now removed the blankets from the figures.

Several lamps had been set on stools at the edge of the display, and the flickering light they produced caught the faces of the figures. Everyone nodded approvingly, and there was a murmur of delight as the nativity scene was revealed.

Paul breathed a sigh of relief. He was proud of what he had achieved, and the nativity scene, with its shepherds, kings, angels, and Holy Family, now appeared as a delightful image for everyone to enjoy.

"It's beautiful, Paul," his *mamm* whispered, and a round of applause broke out, as Bishop Beiler smiled approvingly.

"I think we can all agree – it's a fitting reminder of what we celebrate at this time of year. *Denke*, Paul, for all your hard work," he said, and another round of applause rang out.

Paul did not like being the center of attention, but he was glad the unveiling was over, and as the audience dispersed, he summoned the courage to speak with Barbara and ask her how her sister was faring.

"Congratulations, Paul. You must be so proud," Barbara said, as Paul came up to them.

He smiled, feeling somewhat embarrassed at the adulation he was receiving. Carpentry was his job, and he had taken the task very seriously. He did not like to tell Barbara he had based the face of Mary on her sister, still wondering what Miriam must think of him.

"I wanted to ask how Miriam's doing," he said, just as Susanna and Anna Troyer came over to join them.

"She's doing well. It's a mild concussion. Her headache's gone now, and Doctor Yoder's taken off the bandage from her head. She looks well," Barbara replied.

"But she's been asking about you, Paul. She was disappointed not to be here tonight and see the figures," Susanna said, with slight reproach in her voice.

"I... well, I've had a lot to do. I'm sorry," he said, and Barbara smiled.

"Well, perhaps now's the time to visit. You could fix the chicken coop for her. If you've got time, that is?" she said.

Paul glanced at his *mamm*, who had also come to join the conversation. He was expecting her to mention the fence, which was still to be repaired, but instead, she nodded and smiled at the other members of the quilting circle.

"I think that's an excellent idea. You can do that, can't you, Paul?" she said, and it seemed Paul had no choice but to agree.

He was happy to do so, even as he still feared Miriam's true feelings over what he had done. He had made a promise to her and having failed to fulfill that promise, a terrible accident had occurred. Repairing the chicken coop now felt like closing the stable door after the horse had bolted. But he would do so if it meant making some small amends for what he had done.

"I'd be happy to do so," Paul said.

"Then that's settled then. I'll tell my *mamm* and *daed* to expect you," Barbara said.

"He'll be there tomorrow," Sylvia replied, and the matter was settled.

Paul was left standing by the nativity scene. He looked at the face of Mary, looking down on the infant Jesus lying in the straw. She looked beautiful, and Paul's mind was turned to Miriam.

I hope she realizes I never meant this to happen, he thought to himself, still feeling guilty over what happened, even as he felt determined to make amends.

CHAPTER FOURTEEN

It was Christmas Eve, and Miriam was feeling somewhat sorry for herself. Doctor Yoder had confined her to the house, and with a bump to the head and a sprained wrist, she was unable to do much more than allow herself to be taken care of by her *mamm* and Barbara. They were taking turns acting as nursemaids.

Miriam had just enjoyed a bowl of chicken soup and dumplings and was sitting up in bed, reading a book. She was not particularly concentrating on it, her mind else-where. She had been sorry to miss the Christmas pageant, and sorrier still not to have received a visit from Paul.

"Are you all finished, Miriam?" her *mamm* asked, appearing at the door of Miriam's bedroom.

"I am, *denke, Mamm*. That was delicious soup," she said.

"It always makes me feel better, it was my *mamm's* recipe. She used a certain blend of herbs. It's got to be exact. A pinch of this, a pinch of that. I'll show you how to make it when you're better. It's about time it got passed on," she said.

Miriam had not known her *grossmammi* – she had died before Miriam was born – but the soup had been delicious, and she would be only too pleased to learn the recipe.

"I'm just sorry I feel so useless. I should be helping you with the Christmas baking or bringing in wood for the stove – all that kind of thing," Miriam said, sighing to herself as she lay back on her pillows.

A pleasant scent of Christmas baking – cinnamon, nutmeg, ginger, and cloves – had wafted up the stairs that morning. It was Miriam's favorite time of year, and she felt sad not to be joining in with everything that was happening.

"We can manage. Elijah brought in the wood, and the twins helped with the baking," Lavinia said, smiling at Miriam.

It didn't matter, Miriam would still much rather be doing anything other than lying on her bed pretending to read a book.

"I'll get up later. I can't lie here on Christmas Eve. I want to be downstairs," Miriam said.

Her *mamm* raised her hand. "Not just yet, Miriam," she said, and her tone was firm.

Miriam sighed and nodded. "All right, I'll stay here. But I won't like it," she replied.

Sylvia laughed. "Just stay here a little longer," she said, as a knock came at the door.

Sylvia smiled and left to answer it, leaving Miriam alone. She thought again of Paul, wondering what he was doing, and lamenting the fact she would not be helping Sylvia with her preparations for Christmas.

She had been looking forward to cooking for Paul and his *mamm*, and to helping them celebrate Christmas. She hoped they would manage and wondered if she might ask her own *mamm* to invite them to spend the day with them tomorrow.

It was already set to be a sizable gathering, and two more would not make a difference, given the gargantuan portions usually prepared. But her thoughts of the invitation were distracted by the arrival of Sarah Beiler, who had come bearing a gift of cinnamon cookies for the patient.

"That's so kind of you, *denke*," Miriam said as the bishop's *fraa* set them down on the bedside table.

"Whenever I'm feeling under the weather, a couple of cookies and a cup of warm milk always makes me feel better," Sarah said, smiling at Miriam, who nodded.

"It makes me feel better, too, *denke*," she said as Sarah pulled up a chair at her bedside.

"I was sorry you didn't make the pageant. You'd have loved to have seen the performance. It's one of my favorite times of the year," she said.

Miriam gave a wistful smile. "I wanted to be there. I wanted to see the nativity scene. Paul's worked so hard on it – and so have you and the other ladies," Miriam replied.

She had been thinking a lot about the nativity scene and praying, too. Miriam was not always very *gut* at saying her prayers, but Christmas was always a time when she felt close to her faith and embraced by the love which that nativity scene represented.

"It looked beautiful. He did a wonderful job," Sarah replied.

"I know it sounds selfish – he's had a lot of other things to do. But I hoped he might have come and seen me," Miriam said.

She knew it sounded foolish. She had no right to expect a visit from Paul, but part of her felt sad that she had not seen him, and she had begun to wonder what their fledgling friendship had meant to him.

On her part, she had grown close to him, and there was no doubting the attraction she felt for him. It was for this reason his absence was bitter, even as she knew she should not expect anything from him.

"It's not selfish at all, Miriam. You've grown close to him, haven't you?" Sarah replied.

Miriam nodded. She had grown close to Paul, even as it seemed he had not felt the same. She thought again of Sylvia's curious words about Paul feeling himself to blame for her accident. But there was no blame felt on her part. The chicken coop had fallen down in the wind because Miriam had been too headstrong and had tried to repair it herself. That had been a mistake, and now she was paying for it.

"I thought so. I hoped so," she replied, and Sarah patted her arm.

"It'll be all right. You just rest now, and I'm sure it'll be a happy Christmas," she said, rising to her feet.

She left Miriam alone, closing the bedroom door gently behind her, as Miriam yawned and closed her eyes. She was disturbed by the sound of banging coming from outside – someone was hammering wood, and she rolled her eyes, imagining it was her *daed* trying to repair the chicken coop. But Miriam was beginning to have second thoughts about keeping chickens and wondered if she would be better off without her flock, given the disasters which had already occurred.

"What's all that banging going on outside? *Daed's* not trying to repair the chicken coop, is he?" Miriam asked when her *mamm* entered the room a short while later.

She smiled at Miriam and shook her head.

"You can get up now, Miriam," she said, and Miriam looked at her with confusion.

Earlier, her *mamm* had not allowed her to lift a finger, and now she was telling her she could get up. Miriam had been in bed since the accident, and now she sat up cautiously, swinging her legs over the side of the bed, and testing her balance on the floor.

"I don't want to get into trouble with Doctor Yoder," Miriam said, though she did not feel in the least bit dizzy.

With a secretive smile, her *mamm* helped her stand up without difficulty.

"You won't get into any trouble. I'll help you get dressed," her *mamm* replied.

Miriam was finding this behavior all very odd, but her *mamm* would say nothing more, even as Miriam could see how hard she was trying to disguise the smile on her face.

"Is this something to do with the banging?" Miriam asked.

Her *mamm* shook her head.

"I just thought you'd like to come downstairs. Your sister's there, and you said yourself, you don't want to stay up here all the time. You can help the *kinner* cut out cookies, or just sit by the stove and talk to your *daed*," she said.

Miriam was not about to argue with this newfound declaration of freedom, and she finished dressing herself, relieved at having not felt dizzy in the process.

"I'm ready, I think," she said, and her *mamm* beamed at her.

"Come on then, take my arm. Let's go downstairs," she said, and still feeling somewhat suspicious, Miriam followed.

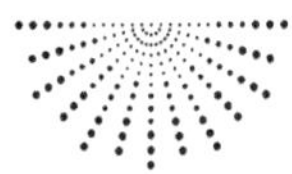

CHAPTER FIFTEEN

*M*iriam went downstairs with only a little difficulty. The bump on her head still hurt a little, and she was slightly unsteady on her feet, but as she came down into the parlor, Miriam was surprised by the sight of several members of the quilting circle there to greet her. Anna Troyer, Sarah Beiler, Sylvia, Susanna, and her sister, all of whom turned to her and smiled.

"Oh, I didn't realize we were having a party," she said, as the women came to greet her.

"Your *mamm* was kind enough to invite us for coffee and cake," Anna said, as Miriam sat down on a chair by the stove.

Her *mamm* came to wrap a blanket around her shoulders, and Miriam was presented with a cup of coffee, and a slice of plum cake.

"That's very kind of you all," she said, smiling at them.

"We wanted you to have a happy Christmas," Sylvia said, even as Miriam felt she had spoiled the Christmas of Paul and his *mamm*.

She was uncertain why the women had come – as kind as it was. They had already visited her, and she was now back on her feet.

"That's very kind of you," Miriam repeated.

The women glanced at one another, and it seemed to Miriam as though they were keeping something back from her. Another loud bang came from outside, and Miriam jumped, almost spilling her coffee as she did so.

"What on earth is going on out there?" she asked, glancing towards the window.

Her *mamm* went to look, glancing back and shaking her head.

"It's just your *daed*. He'll be done in a few minutes, I'm sure," she said, pulling the curtain across the window.

Something strange was going on, but Miriam knew she would not be privy to it until her *mamm* decided the time was right. The other women, too, seemed to know what was going on, they all had those secret grins where you are trying to hide a smile. It made the conversation forced for the next few minutes, as the women made extensive inquiries as to Miriam's health.

"You've come through it, though," Anna said, smiling at Miriam, who nodded.

"It could've been a lot worse. I'm just grateful to Doctor Yoder for patching me up," she said.

"You've got to be so careful out in the snow. I once slipped on the porch, and Paul had to pick me up," Sylvia said, shaking her head.

The mention of Paul caused Miriam's heart to skip a beat. She wanted to ask Sylvia why her son had not come to visit. She was beginning to wonder if Paul was afraid of facing up to his feelings – if he had them for Miriam. Once bitten, twice shy.

"Is he... all right?" Miriam asked.

Sylvia looked at her in surprise. "Oh... he's fine, *denke.* Yes, he's quite all right," she said, laughing nervously.

Now Miriam really did know something was going on, but before she could question Sylvia further, her *mamm* gave an exclamation and beckoned her to the window, the curtain of which she had just pulled back. It was early afternoon, and whilst dusk was settling, there was still enough light to see by.

Barbara helped Miriam to her feet, and filled with curiosity, she made her way to the window, followed by the other women. The parlor window looked out over the garden, and in the fading light, Miriam saw a sight that took her breath away.

"I can't believe it," she exclaimed, as tears welled up in her eyes.

Out in the snow stood Paul. He was leaning next to the chicken coop, which had now been moved, and was surrounded by a high fence with netting. It looked brand new, completely repaired, and with every piece of wood in place. Miriam could not believe it. Paul raised his hand and waved to her shyly. She returned the gesture, and now her *mamm* pointed past Paul, to where another sight caused her to let out an exclamation of astonishment. There, in the snow, were the nativity figures, wearing their costumes, and arranged just like the scene in Bethlehem. Tears rolled down Miriam's cheeks, and she shook her head, hardly able to believe what she was seeing.

"Do you like it?" her *mamm* whispered.

Miriam swallowed down a lump of emotion and nodded. "I think it's wonderful," she replied, hardly daring to believe it was true.

The other women smiled at her, and Miriam felt a sudden urge to go outside and thank Paul for all he had done. He had repaired the chicken coop just as he had promised, and he had brought the nativity to her door. Her *mamm* helped her with her boots, and she put on her *daed's* overcoat, before hurrying out of the house. All thoughts of her condition were gone, and she only wanted to thank Paul for everything he had done for her.

"I hope you like it," Paul said, as he came to meet her by the nativity figures.

"I think it's wonderful," she said, looking around her.

The figures were exquisite, each of them perfectly carved, and Miriam was captivated by their faces, even as they were now disappearing in the gloom of that winter night. But despite the darkness, Miriam could only think of light – the light that came into the world on that first Christmas Day, and which these figures represented.

"And the chicken coop. I promised you I'd mend it," he said.

Miriam smiled. "It's a palace. You even did the fencing, too. Oh, it's just wonderful. I can't wait to put the chickens in there," she said, and Paul laughed.

"Your *daed* already did. We moved them together. They're all roosting inside – safe and sound," he said.

Miriam smiled. "That's so kind of you, Paul. I can't thank you enough," she said, and she put out her hand and touched his arm.

He smiled at her, looking somewhat embarrassed.

"I'm sorry I didn't do it sooner, that's all. I promised you, and I let you down, and then the accident happened, and..." he began, but Miriam interrupted him.

"Is that why you stayed away? Did you think I blamed you for the accident?" she asked.

Paul nodded. The look on his face was one of agony.

CHAPTER SIXTEEN

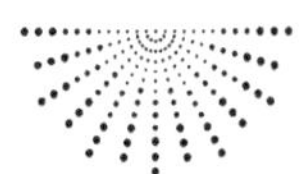

"I thought you'd be angry. My *mamm* tried to tell me you wouldn't be, but..." Paul shrugged. "It was her and the others who asked me to repair the coop. I thought you'd like to see the figures. But... I'm sorry, I didn't think... well, I did think, I thought a lot. I thought you'd be angry with me," he said.

Miriam shook her head. She had never thought to blame Paul for the accident. It was not his fault – none of it. It was only when Sylvia had mentioned it, she had thought of it, and it had never occurred to her to hold Paul in any way responsible.

"You don't need to think like that, please... it's not your fault. I'm not angry with you. I should've done a better job of repairing the coop myself. It was probably my fiddling with it that made the slats of wood loose in the first place. There was a gust of wind. I was standing in the wrong place at the wrong time. I shouldn't have been out there in that kind of weather. Your *mamm* mentioned something about you feeling guilty but is that why you stayed away?" she asked.

Paul nodded. He looked sheepish, and Miriam shook her head and sighed.

"I was more upset because you didn't come and see me. Did you stay away because you thought I'd be angry with you?" she asked.

Again, Paul nodded.

"I've messed up, haven't I? It's just... after Sally, I'm not very *gut* at reading the signs. I never knew what I did to make her behave like that. It felt like she hated me, and I couldn't understand why. I was terrified you'd feel the same way. I didn't want it to be like that with you. I thought I'd made a terrible mistake," he said.

Miriam shook her head.

Paul was not to blame for what had happened, nor would Miriam do so. She *had* been upset, but not because she blamed him for the accident. It was his staying away, which had confused her. She had wanted him to come, and she had felt sad when he did not.

"You didn't make a mistake – except for staying away," she said.

Paul hung his head. "I'm sorry. I just don't have any confidence anymore. I've vowed never... well, after Sally. Oh, I'm not doing very well, am I?" he said.

Miriam reached out and took his hand in hers. "*Nee*, you're not, but I'm sure you can do better," she said, smiling at him.

He returned her smile, even as he still looked thoroughly embarrassed.

"It's just... well, I wasn't expecting to meet someone like you. After Sally, I thought all women were the same. I couldn't trust anyone. I didn't want my heart broken again. I was wary. But you're different. You're nothing like Sally, or anyone else. You're just, you," he said, shaking his head, as though he could not quite believe what he was saying.

Miriam's heart skipped a beat, and she squeezed his hand, even as she shivered against the cold. She felt just the same about him, too. He had entered her life entirely unexpectedly, and she could not help but feel a sense of

Gott's guiding hand in what they had shared. Her feelings for him were in no doubt, and she smiled up at him, their eyes meeting in a loving gaze.

"I know you got hurt, Paul. But I won't hurt you. I'm not going anywhere. I wanted you to come to me, and now you have – you've brought me a chicken coop and a nativity scene. What more could I ask for? I never blamed you for the accident. I didn't expect you to repair the chicken coop when you had the figures to finish – not to mention your *mamm's* fence," she said, and Paul laughed.

"I've still not fixed the fence," he said, shaking his head.

"Then you'd better get on with it. I've got my Christmas present. Your *mamm* needs hers. But I'm so grateful to you. I'm so glad we could share this moment. I just wish you hadn't stayed away," she said, squeezing his hand once again.

"I promise I won't do. Not anymore. If that's what you want, that is. I hope I haven't spoiled things," he said, but Miriam shook her head.

She could not be angry with him – there was no reason to be. She had fallen in love with him, and that was all that mattered.

"Stop apologizing for things you haven't done," she said, and he smiled at her.

It was almost dark now, but the moon had come out from behind a cloud, its light catching the snow, which sparkled like a million diamonds.

"All right, I promise – no more apologies," he said, and she smiled back at him.

"Come on, let's go inside. It's getting cold out here," she said, and she led him onto the porch and into the parlor.

The others had moved back from the window and were sitting around the table, drinking coffee and eating pieces of stolen cake fresh from the oven. They looked up as Miriam and Paul entered the parlor, and Miriam's *mamm* smiled at her.

"Are you pleased with your new chicken coop, Miriam?" she asked.

Miriam smiled so brightly she feared her face would split.

"Very pleased, *denke*. It's wonderful. And what a wonderful way to begin the celebrations by having the nativity brought to me," she said, and the others smiled.

"We'll have to take it back at some point, but the Bishop says it can stay there for tomorrow," Sarah Beiler said.

Miriam and Paul sat down at the table, and cups of coffee and pieces of cake were passed to them. Miriam could not have felt happier, and as they sat and talked, she realized she had found her place in Faith's Creek – she had friends now, and a purpose, not to mention her fledgling romance.

"I've invited Paul and Sylvia for Christmas Day. That means we'll have a full house – there'll be you, your *daed*, and I. Barbara, Elijah, and the twins, Susanna, and Paul and Sylvia," Miriam's *mamm* said, and Miriam smiled.

"I think that's a wonderful idea," she said.

"I asked Anna and Sarah, but they've got their own families, of course," Miriam's *mamm* continued.

"It's very kind of you, Lavinia, but we'll be sure to call in over the holiday period," Sarah Beiler said, rising to her feet.

Anna joined her, and the two of them wished the others goodbye and a very happy Christmas. The scene was set for the happiest of days, and when Paul and Sylvia left, it was with the promise of returning very soon.

"After the morning service – and make sure you come hungry," Lavinia said, as they said goodbye.

Miriam smiled at Paul, who blushed under her gaze.

"I'll see you tomorrow," she said, and he nodded.

"I'll be here – I promise," he said, and Miriam pointed to the snowflake ornament hanging in the window.

"It's my favorite decoration," she said, as she bid him goodnight.

"Wasn't that a lovely thing to do?" Barbara said, as she closed the door and turned to the others.

Miriam still could not believe what had happened, and she sat by the stove, hardly noticing her injuries. For the first time in a very long time, Miriam felt happy. She was surrounded by her family and was building a future for herself.

"It was so kind," she said, and for the rest of the evening, all she could think about was seeing Paul again, and sharing the happiness she had found.

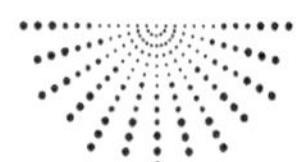

CHAPTER SEVENTEEN

"*K*inner who eat well are always welcome at my table. Aren't they marvels?" Lavinia said, fussing over the twins, who had just finished two enormous pieces of shoofly pie.

The table was still heaving, despite the valiant attempts of the guests to devour everything laid before them. Lavinia had outdone herself, and the turkey had been the moistest and most succulent anyone had ever tasted.

"It's been a triumph, Lavinia," Sylvia said, raising a glass of apple juice in a toast.

"Absolutely," Paul said, sitting back with a satisfied sigh.

"And we're only too glad to have shared it with you all," Thomas said.

They had all attended the morning service, where Bishop Beiler had preached an inspiring sermon on the meaning of that first Christmas, reminding the congregation that *Gott* became poor so that we could become rich with His blessings.

"It's normally just the two of us for Christmas, isn't it, Paul? It was hard work last year. I like to do things properly, but this is just wonderful," Sylvia said, beaming around the table.

Miriam rose to help her *mamm* begin clearing away the plates, as did Barbara, and the three women retreated to the kitchen.

"You don't have to do this," Barbara said, ushering Miriam out.

"But I want to. I'm tired of being waited on hand and foot," she replied, but Barbara laughed.

"Now you're getting a taste of your own medicine. You didn't let me lift a finger when I was recovering from my accident," she said, and Miriam smiled.

"All right, I suppose so," she said, and she returned to the parlor.

The twins were playing with their newly acquired toys, and Thomas had retreated to his favorite chair, where he was now dozing contentedly. Sylvia and Susanna were discussing patterns for a new quilt, and Elijah had been called by Barbara to help with the dishes.

"I feel like I should be helping, too," Paul said, rising from his place, but Miriam shook her head.

"You worked hard yesterday, and I've been told – in no uncertain terms – I'm not to lift a finger. But we could have a walk in the snow. I'd like to look at the nativity figures again. It was hard to see them properly in the gloom yesterday evening," she said.

Paul thought that was a very *gut* idea, and they were soon bundled up against the cold and stepping out onto the porch. The clouds had cleared, leaving behind a bright, sunny day, though the air was freezing cold. Miriam was glad of her overcoat, and the scarf she had wrapped over her *kapp* and round her head. Paul offered her his arm, and she stepped down from the porch into the snow, her foot disappearing, as she let out a cry.

"Careful, it's deep," he said, as he caught hold of her.

She looked up at him and smiled, and the two of them walked arm in arm around the side of the house, to where the chicken coop stood. Miriam's *daed* had let the hens out that morning, and they were scratching in the snow, clucking, and brooding. Miriam liked to watch them. She had several pretty breeds, their feathers standing out colorfully against the white blanket of snow. But it was the nativity figures she had come to see, and now she turned to examine them, marveling at the beauty of the costumes, and the intricate carvings of the faces.

"I think they're wonderful. They'll last for years, won't they?" she said, and Paul nodded.

"I hope so. Long after I'm gone. I like to think of them being used year by year. It's such a special time, and it's so important to keep traditions alive – the pageant, the nativity scene, and coming together as a family. That's what our way of life's all about – tradition, and I'm proud to be a part of that," he said.

Miriam had stooped down to examine the faces more carefully, and she ran her fingers along the virgin Mary's hairline, finding something familiar in the facial features.

"I think she's my favorite," she said, looking up at Paul, whom she was surprised to see was blushing.

"She's my favorite, too. I didn't tell you this yesterday, but her face... it's your face," he said.

Miriam stared at him in surprise, before turning back to the figure, and recognizing herself immediately.

Tears filled her eyes, and she shook her head, hardly able to believe he had done something so meaningful for her. It was the most wonderful gift and he kneeled down in the snow next to her and put his arm around her.

"I don't know what to say... my face. I can see it now. It's so beautiful, Paul. *Denke – denke* from the bottom of my heart. I didn't know if I'd fit into Faith's Creek. But you've made sure I'm right at the heart of this community," she said, slipping her hand into his.

"I was finding the face the hardest part. I kept trying to get it right, but I didn't have an idea of how I wanted it to be. Then... I just had an inspiration, as though *Gott* gave me the solution in you. I think perhaps... *Gott* gave me you as the solution to so many of my problems, Miriam," he said.

Miriam turned and smiled at him.

She felt just the same. He had come into her life when she had felt directionless and without purpose. But through meeting him, she had found that direction and purpose, and she could not have felt happier.

"And you're the solution to mine, Paul. Meeting you... working for your *mamm*, keeping the chickens. It feels like everything's fallen into place. I didn't know where I was going, or what I was doing, but you changed that," she said, squeezing his hand.

"And where are we going?" he asked, gazing into her eyes.

Miriam smiled. She was not sure exactly where they were going, only that she was willing to set out on the journey, confident of a happy ending. She had fallen in love with him, and he had fallen in love with her. That was the beginning of the journey – love. Love was the beginning of so many journeys, and the carved figure of the baby lying in the manger was proof of that. Love did not need to be complicated. It only needed two hearts to become one – that was enough.

"Wherever we're going, I hope it's together," she said, and he nodded.

"I'd like that, too. I love you. You are the most caring person I've ever met," he said, and leaning forward, he kissed her, as her arms slipped around his waist.

At that moment, Miriam realized where happiness lay – it was right here, in Paul's arms, and she could not have felt happier. As their lips parted, she sat back in the snow and smiled.

"I love you too. We've got so much to look forward to, haven't we? Promise you won't ever stay away again?" she said, and he nodded.

"I promise – if only to keep you from carpentry disasters," he said, and Miriam laughed.

"I'll leave the carpentry to you," she replied, and taking her in his arms, he kissed her again, as the happiness of that Christmas Day brought them both the joy they deserved.

They sat in the snow, holding each other as they stared at the nativity scene and understood what Christmas was all about.

If you enjoyed this book you will love An Amish Christmas Blessing

5 AMISH BROTHERS
AN AMISH CHRISTMAS
Blessing
SARAH MILLER
kindleunlimited

CHRISTMAS BRIDES AND SEASONAL WISHES – PREVIEW

FAITH'S CREEK, PENNSYLVANIA

The snow was mesmerizing, falling from the inky dark sky above and blanketing the garden in a pristine covering. The fields around the house appeared as a single expanse of white as far as the eye could see.

Beth Phillips stood at the window, looking out. She had been standing there for an hour or so, just watching the snow fall, thinking of nothing in particular. She liked winter, the warm fires and the cozy nights, the prospect of Christmas to come – though, for her, the season was always twinged with sadness.

It was December, and the first snows had hit hard that year, the ground frozen and the roads around Faith's

Creek icy and treacherous. But Beth had no reason to venture out, the smell of a casserole bubbling on the stove, and the crackle of logs on the fire kept her company as she waited for Isaac's return.

She sighed and pulled the curtain across the window, turning back into the parlor to check all was ready for her husband's arrival. As she did so, she caught sight of herself in the mirror by the porch door. Her long brown hair, always covered by her kapp when outside was hanging down over her shoulders, her wide blue eyes filled with tears.

"You need to cheer up before Isaac comes home," she told herself.

The house was pristine – there was no reason for it not to be. Each morning, after she bid goodbye to Isaac, sending him off to the blacksmith's store with a packet of sandwiches and a flask of coffee, she would make the bed, tidy the parlor, clean down the stove and work her way through a myriad of jobs which designed not only to ensure domestic harmony but also to provide distraction. The house was quiet. It was missing the one thing Beth desired more than anything else in the world: the sound of *kinner*.

The couple had been married for five years, and in those five years, Beth had conceived three times. Each occasion had been a cause for joy and celebration, and each had ended in bitter sorrow and disappointment. There were three *kinner* in Beth's heart, three *kinner* who should have been there now, their voices filling the house, which felt so empty. Every little sound was magnified, not only by the silence of that winter afternoon, but the silence Beth felt at being alone. Each *kinner* had been conceived in love, and each was lost, at rest with *Gott*, and leaving behind it a restless heart in Beth, and a deep sorrow, too.

She longed for a *kinner* to call her own, to hold, and to be a *mamm* to. The names of those three *kinner* were etched on her heart Elijah, Reuben, and Jonah – she thought of each of them every day, and now she glanced across at the mantelpiece, where always she kept three candles burning, one for each of the *kinner* she had lost. A tear ran down her cheek, and she scolded herself for allowing her emotions to overwhelm her. What sort of welcome would that be for Isaac, who was due home at any moment? She did not want him to see she had been crying, and she pulled out her handkerchief and wiped her eyes, just as footsteps on the porch announced his return.

"What a day, it's really come in bad," Isaac said, stomping his boots on the mat, so that the snow flew in white specs on the rug, melting as they hit.

"Oh, well, come inside and warm up. I've just put more wood on the fire. There's a casserole on the stove top, too. You'll soon warm up. How was your day?" Beth asked, coming to kiss him, and taking his hat and coat.

He was a handsome man, four years older than her, with dark hair and dark eyes, and a face which always seemed to smile. Beth loved him with all her heart, and that only magnified the sorrow she felt at not being able to give him the one thing she knew he desired above all else.

"It was all right, but we're going to be hard-pressed to finish the plow repairs for Daniel Graeber before Christmas. He wants the whole thing: stripping back, new parts – we might as well build him a new plow as repair the old one," Isaac replied, pulling off his boots and coming to sit by the fire.

Beth smiled, hoping he would not notice she had been crying. It was the same every day lately. As Christmas approached, she found herself thinking more and more about what they had lost. The house where they lived was close to the schoolhouse, and each morning, Beth would endure the sight of parents taking their little one there, the happy smiles on their faces, the shouts and cries, the laughter – she longed to share in all of that, for she had seen many of her friends become parents and knew the joy their *kinner* brought them.

"I'm sure you'll get it all done. Do you want a drink? Something hot, perhaps? I tried that recipe for mulled apple juice Sarah Beiler gave me. It's delicious," she said.

Isaac nodded. "What did I ever do to deserve you?" he said, smiling at her.

Beth blushed. She did not think herself deserving of Isaac. They had been childhood sweethearts, insepara-ble, and there had been little doubt in anyone's mind that they would marry. On that happy day, the world had seemed so full of possibility, and they had dreamed of starting a family together. But as the candles on the mantelpiece testified, such dreams had come to nothing. Theirs was a quiet house, and Beth longed for the one thing she could not have – a *kinner* of her own to fill the house with noise.

"I'll just see to the casserole," she said, retreating to the kitchen, as she felt fresh tears welling up in her eyes.

She ladled a cup of the mulled apple juice into a mug, setting it on the side, as she glanced out of the window across the darkening garden which backed onto their neighbor's yard. The Hochstetler's had built a snowman below their porch, with twigs for arms and pieces of coal running up its front as buttons, a carrot was stuck in for a nose, and pebbles made a smiling face and eyes, one of Moses Hochstetler's old hats was pulled down low over its head. She thought of the *kinner* at play, and she reached out and pulled the curtain quickly across the window lest her thoughts overwhelm her once more.

"Are you all right?" Isaac asked, and she jumped, not realizing he had entered the kitchen.

"Oh... I'm all right, it's just getting dark," she said, forcing her face into a smile, and turning to pass him the mug of mulled apple juice.

"And cold, I think we're in for a harsh winter," he said, taking the mug and holding it in both hands.

Beth nodded. She was not sure how much longer she could keep up her charade. Every day it grew harder to put on a brave face and say the right things. Inside, she was hurting, and she had no one but Isaac to confide in. He was so kind and worked tirelessly to provide for her. She felt guilty at the thought of adding to his worries, and she knew he was hurting, too. He did not speak of it, but the pain was clear to see. Sometimes, she would find him staring at the three lit candles, with a look of such sorrow on his face that it broke her heart to see.

"Last year was so mild, it's like the weather's making up for it. It's been years since we've had such snows here," Beth replied, taking the casserole off the stove.

"Maybe we should build a snowman, too," he said, smiling at her, and Beth laughed, remembering happier days when the winter would bring sledding and snowball fights.

The past was a far happier place than the present for Beth, and she would often allow her mind to wander, remembering fondly what had been.

"Let's eat," she said, taking two plates from the cupboard and ladling out the casserole.

Grab this amazing box set - 26 Christmas Brides and Seasonal Wishes for FREE with Kindle Unlimited

26
Book
Box Set
INDIANA WAKE, SARAH MILLER,
BELLE FIFFER, CHARLOTTE DARCY
& ROSIE SAMS
CHRISTMAS BRIDES
AND
Seasonal Wishes
unlimited

The Amish Family and Faith Collection

Find all Sarah's books on Amazon and click the yellow follow button

This book is dedicated to the wonderful Amish people and the faithful life that they live.

Go in peace, my friends.

As an independent author, Sarah relies on your support. If you enjoyed this book, please leave a review on Amazon or Goodreads.

ABOUT THE AUTHOR

Sarah Miller was born in Pennsylvania and spent her childhood close to the Amish people. Weekends were spent doing chores; quilting or eventually babysitting in the community. She grew up to love their culture and the simple lifestyle and had many Amish friends. The one thing that you can guarantee when you are near the Amish, Sarah believes is that you will feel close to God.

Many years later she married Martin who is the love of her life and moved to England. There she started to write stories about the Amish. Recently after a lot of persuasion from her best friend she has decided to publish her stories. They draw on inspiration from her relationship with the Amish and with God and she hopes you enjoy reading them as much as she did writing them. Many of the stories are based on true events but names have been changed and even though they are authentic at times artistic license has been used.

Sarah likes her stories simple and to hold a message and they help bring her closer to her faith. She currently lives in Yorkshire, England with her husband Martin and seven very spoiled chickens.

She would love to meet you on Facebook at https://www.facebook.com/SarahMillerBooks

Sarah hopes her stories will both entertain and inspire and she wishes that you go with God.